AINSLEY

THE MIXOLOGY SERIES

KRISSY V

This one's for my mum. A strong woman who loves hard!

BUBBLY BAHAMA

Half a glass of champagne, 25ml peach schnapps, 10ml apple schnapps, Top up with 7Up, grenadine, lime to garnish and rimming sugar

Keaton and Dakota left this morning. I know we're going to see them soon, but it was really emotional saying goodbye. I love Dakota like a sister, and Keaton is okay as a brother, I guess. I'm hoping we can all go out and watch the World Surfing Championship in Australia, but I'm not sure we can all go because of Mixology. We'll have to wait and see. I'm sitting at the breakfast table, looking out at the sea. I love the sea; it's so calming and it reminds me of my childhood.

With my hands wrapped around my coffee, I laugh as I remember telling Scarlett, Dakota, and Issy that I've told the boys I prefer girls. They've become so overprotective. They were always bad when we were growing up, but now it's out of hand. I can't have any dates because they find out about them. It's driving me insane. I've even gone so far as thinking of hiring a prostitute because I seriously need to get laid.

I can't dwell on it though, as there is a lot of paperwork to do in Mixology. With Keaton leaving, the extra work needs to be spread out, with Hunter taking on some extra jobs, and Scarlett and I doing extra admin.

I love working with Scarlett. We always have so much fun and her relationship with Hunter is really strong; they're well-suited. I'm happy they got together, even with what happened with Finn.

"Hey, Scarlett," I say, flinging my bag down on the desk. "What do we need to do today?"

"There's some bills that need paying and some orders that need placing. We've been really busy lately so we're going to have to chip in with bar work as well now that Dakota and Keaton have left us."

"Right. Let's write some lists and see how we get on with them."

I love lists. I write lists of lists that need to be written.

When the delivery comes, I rush outside.

"Hey, Rod. How's things?" I say. He's sexy, in a dirty kind of way.

"Hey, Ainsley. Better now I've seen you," he says, picking up two of the barrels and carrying them on his shoulders so I can see his muscles rippling.

Hunter comes outside. "Ains, we'll organise the delivery. You can go back inside."

"No, it's fine. I just want to check some stuff with Rod. You can go back in. It's fine, really."

He is pissing me off now. I've been trying to talk to Rod for weeks, but every time he's here, one of my brothers comes out and takes over.

"Ains."

"Oh, for God's sake!" Stamping my feet, I storm back into Mixology.

Scarlett laughs when I stomp into the office and slam the door. She knows exactly what has just happened. "I think you need to ramp up operation lesbian."

"Who are you telling? I need sex, Scarlett. Like, seriously need it. I'm sick of using my vibrator all the time. Me and Porn Hub have a special relationship."

Scarlett is rolling around laughing. I think I even see tears in her eyes.

The door opens and Issy walks in. "What did I miss, girls?"

"Ainsley was just telling me that she needs sex and is fed up of using her vibrator!"

"Oh my God, no way! Ainsley, I can fix you up with someone if you want. I have some connections down at The Underground!"

"Really? That would be awesome." Smiling at her, I feel like she could be my saviour. I'm not fussy at this stage.

Scarlett laughs and bangs the table. "Erm, did you forget Zac goes down there? There is no chance he is going to let you hook up with anyone from The Underground, Ainsley. No way in hell!"

"Fuck. I didn't think of that. Right, I'm starting operation lesbian tonight. I've had enough. Then I'm going to find some guy who doesn't come here and doesn't know any of my brothers. Don't ask me how I'm going to do it, because I don't know myself. But I'm sure I can write a list for it."

The three of us break down laughing.

The boys come in. "What's going on here?" Zac wraps his arm around Issy and pulls her close.

"You don't want to know, pretty boy!" She leans her head on his chest and I'm sure I see her breathe him in.

I think it's hilarious that he lets her get away with calling him *pretty boy*. Keaton tried it one day and Zac tackled him to the floor.

Zac picks Issy up and kisses her. He has no shame; he even touches her arse in front of us. I want to be sick because he's my brother, but damn, it's still kind of hot.

Scarlett watches me and shakes her head, laughing.

"Fuck you all." Storming out of the office, I hope they all go to hell.

It's busy tonight, and Zac's working with me at the front door. A couple of guys try to hit on me and he cock blocks them every time.

When the door opens the next time, it's my best friend, Callie. "Hey, Ainsley. You're looking hot tonight." She looks me up and down. Callie is a lesbian and she's gorgeous. If I really was that way inclined then I would want to go out with her.

Now, there's a thought. I pull her in for a hug. "Hey, Callie. Not looking so bad yourself."

She smiles. "Anything happening in there tonight?"

"Not yet. I'll be on a break soon, so I'll come in and have a drink with you."

"Great. See you soon, babe." She kisses me on the cheek and Zac opens the door for her.

"She's gorgeous, Ainsley. Shame she likes girls," he says.

"What do you mean *a shame*? I didn't class you as homophobic, Zac. And also, you have a girlfriend!'"

"I'm not. I'm just saying it's a waste for the guys who would be lucky to take her home."

"What would you think if I said I was a lesbian?"

"I see you going after Rod, Ains. That's not a sign of a lesbian."

"I'm just being nice to him." I wait for a few minutes, and then, smiling at him, I say, "She's hot though, right?"

He laughs at me.

We're busy for the next hour, then I tell Zac I'm going for my break. "See you in a bit. I'll bring you back coffee." I have to keep him sweet and he loves coffee.

When I open the door, the first thing I hear is the music playing loud. Skylar plays some great tunes. He looks over and waves at me, and I wave back.

Seeing Callie, I head straight over to her. "How's things? Anything happening?"

"Not much. What's going on?" She knows me well enough to know I have a lot on my mind.

I sit down at the table next to her. My heart rate has spiked and I'm worried she'll turn me down. I know the best way is just to ask her, like pulling a band-aid off in one go. "I'm having problems with my brothers."

"What's new?"

"Listen, I really hate to ask this, but would you do me a favour and pretend to be my girlfriend? I need to get my brothers off my back. I know it's a lot to ask."

She starts laughing. "Are you serious?" She looks me in the eye. Yeah, she can see I'm being serious. "Look, Ainsley, I love you, you know that, but I'm not sure about this. They won't believe it's real. We've been friends for years and we've never kissed. Why would you start having feelings for me? It doesn't make sense to me and it won't make sense to them."

"You know I wouldn't ask if I wasn't serious. They just won't back off. I told them I like girls, but now I need to back it up. I can't think of anyone I would rather be in a fake relationship with." I smile and flutter my eyelashes, hoping that will work."

"God, Ainsley, don't look at me like that. You know I find it hard to say no to you when you look at me with those puppy dog eyes."

"What puppy dog eyes?" I look up from under my lashes and flutter them again. "Oh, you mean these…"

Callie starts laughing. She sounds frustrated when a growl comes out of her mouth. "You won't freak out if I touch you? It won't work if you do." She reaches across the table and takes my hand. "Do you want to kiss me and stuff?"

"I… I hadn't really thought it through, to be honest. I want it to be believable, so yeah. Touch me and kiss me." I'm not really sure how I feel about kissing another girl, but she's my best friend and she's gorgeous. So who better than Callie?

She's quiet for a few minutes and I'm sure the cogs are turning in her mind while she thinks about it. "Okay, I'll do it," she says, laughing. "This is going to be fun. I can't wait to see their faces."

I'm delighted she said yes, but I'm so apprehensive about kissing her in front of my brothers. Taking a deep breath, I hug her. "Thanks, babe. I need to get Zac his coffee or he will be like a bear with a sore head."

Laughing, she pulls away from me. "Just a quick kiss to get them started." She doesn't wait for me to answer as she kisses me on the lips. Winking, she lets me go. I shake my head, laughing as I go out to the kitchen to make coffee. I just hope I know what I'm doing.

The door flies open and Hunter comes rushing in. "Did I see you kiss Callie?"

Oh, God. Already?

"Yeah. I told you I like girls."

"I didn't think you meant it!" He shakes his head. "At least that's better than a guy, and Callie's stunning and so much fun too."

"It's early days yet. Don't tell Mum and Dad." I'm not sure how I feel about them thinking I'm into girls. They're open-minded, but that might just push them too far.

"I won't. Scarlett saw you and told me so she knows too."

"Listen, Hunter, people are going to see us. We've nothing to hide."

"I know, Ains." He pulls me against him in a hug.

"I've got to take this coffee to Zac. You know what he's like without his coffee." I laugh.

Hunter smiles at me and leaves the kitchen. I make the coffee and take it back out to Zac.

About an hour later, Callie's comes out. "Hey, babe." She stands next to me and touches my arm. "Do you want to go somewhere after work?"

"Yeah. Where did you have in mind?"

"I know this club that's open 'til six in the morning."

"Ooh, sounds good to me. I don't have much on tomorrow."

She leans in to me and my heart rate increases. I don't know what she's going to do. "Relax," she whispers, and then she grabs my neck and pulls me close and kisses me. It takes me a couple of moments to recover from the shock, then I see Zac watching us so I kiss her back.

All of a sudden, I hear clapping. "Wow. Now

that's hot!" Zac is staring at us. "I need to find Issy and see if she will kiss another girl for me."

"Fuck off, Zac," Callie says, smiling at me. "I'll be back later when you finish, babe. See you then."

I touch my lips with two fingers. They are swollen from where she kissed me.

EL DIABLO

1 oz frozen limeade, 1 ½ oz tequila blance, ½ oz crème de cassis, ¾ oz still water, 1 ½ oz ginger beer

It's been a week since I asked Callie to act as my girlfriend, and, so far, it's going well. We've convinced my brothers, anyway; that was always going to be the hardest. Except, of course, they are delighted I don't like cock. I laugh because they are so wrong. I love cock and need to get some soon or I will seriously think about being a lesbian for real.

Callie is gorgeous and she kisses so well that it's easy to be swept away. Even when we go clubbing after work, we still kiss, just in case there are any of my brother's spies watching.

It's Wednesday night and I'm working, of

course. Callie comes in early. She hugs me and kisses me intensely. It's so funny when we pull apart, because Zac is always watching. When we part, she turns to Zac. "Are you watching us?"

"So what if I am? It's still hot!" He laughs. "I asked Issy if she'd kiss a girl for me. She wasn't keen. I think I need her to watch you two in action." He laughs and takes out his phone.

A few minutes later, the door to the bar opens and Issy comes out. She surprises me every time I see her. She's tiny, especially in comparison to Zac. "Hey, " she says, smiling at him.

"Princess, you need to hang out here and see these two kissing."

She rolls her eyes. "Seriously? Are you still on this threesome buzz?"

He smiles like a lunatic. "Yeah. What do you think?"

"I told you, I don't share well. If you want me to do a threesome then it has to be with two men, not two women!"

His face drops. "Forget it then."

She stands on her tiptoes. "We have enough fun ourselves. We don't need another woman. I'm enough for you to handle, pretty boy," she says, grabbing his cock.

"Oh my God. Stop that, Issy! I don't need to see my brother's dick in his trousers."

She starts laughing. "Have you got a break now, pretty boy? I think I need to see you in the cellar. There's a barrel that needs changing." She winks at me.

I nod and they both leave.

"That was awkward," Callie says, laughing.

"I know."

"Listen, there's a party tomorrow night that I've been invited to. Do you want to come with me?"

"I'd love to. I'll ask Hunter if I can get the night off, or can we go after work?"

"It starts earlier in the afternoon. They're having a pool party, then there's some food and then the party starts in full swing."

"Okay, sounds great. I'll ask Hunter in a bit." The front door opens and punters keep coming in. It's quite busy for a Wednesday night.

Zac eventually comes back with a big smile on his face. He makes me laugh. He's been so angry for years and I love seeing him this happy. I always thought his and Issy's relationship was toxic and that they shouldn't be together, but once he talked through his problems and his grief, I can see they're perfect together. Their passion is so amazing. I want that one day. I want that for myself.

"I'm going on a break now, Zac," I say.

"Are you going to the cellar too?" he asks, laughing.

I hold my middle finger up to him. He laughs and I walk into the bar.

It's knee deep in punters in here so I get behind the bar and help them out. "Thanks, sis," Hunter says, and we work side by side for an hour.

When it calms down, I leave the bar, but before I do, I ask, "Hey, Hunter. Any chance of having tomorrow night off? I can help Scarlett in the morning and then I have a party to go to."

He eyes me. "Are you going with Callie?"

"Yeah, she is," Callie says, coming up behind me and wrapping her hand around my waist.

He smiles. "Of course you can have the night off. You're always working."

"Thanks, Hunter." I give him a tight squeeze.

"Right, Callie. It's party time tomorrow night."

"Yay," she says.

We go to the kitchen to make coffee and then she says, "Right, I'm going home. I'll see you tomorrow. I'll pick you up at one o'clock."

"One o'clock. Great. Early night for me tonight then."

She kisses me on the cheek and then leaves me in the kitchen. The kettle boils, interrupting my deep thoughts.

I'm excited about the party and can't wait to let my hair down. It's been a while since I've been to a pool party. We used to have them at our house for years and they are so much fun. The weather is supposed to be great tomorrow, so I'd better get my best bikini out when I get home.

I take Zac his coffee and we don't get chance for another break as it's so busy. Busy is good; it means the money is coming in.

Mixology is one of the fastest growing bars in Torquay. It has earned a reputation for a great night out with no trouble. As a family, we all work bloody hard to make it a success. Hunter's ideas from Australia are so different to the way the other bars are run around here. Everyone who comes here knows that it will be nothing like the other cocktail bar in town.

It's half past ten when I wake up. I groan and turn

over. I'm more of a night owl than a morning person, which is why Mixology really suits me. After about ten minutes, I know that I have to get up and get organised. I have my washing to do today and I really need to find that gorgeous peach bikini for the pool party.

After having breakfast, I start on the washing. When all of that is done, I pull out my peach bikini, a sarong to go with it, and then a dress to wear to the party tonight. Putting it all in my bag, I head into the shower, ready to start the day.

Callie comes to pick me up bang on time. She's always punctual, but I am too, so I'm ready and waiting for her. She buzzes and I let her in.

"Morning, babe," she says, kissing me on the cheek. "You're looking good."

I look her up and down. She's wearing a navy and gold bikini and a navy wrap. "Thanks, hun. I love the colour of your sarong."

"Thanks." I grab my bag, and we both sing, "Let's get this party started."

We stop on the way to get some alcohol and then we're ready to head over. The party is in a nice suburb of Torquay, Livermead, where most of the houses are large and have swimming pools. Callie pulls up outside a big house which is at the end of a road, overlooking the cliffs and sea. She parks the car and then we climb out and head to the front door. The door is open and we walk in.

"Whose party is this?" I ask, looking around in awe. Mum and Dad's house is big, but this is like a mansion.

"Some guy. I can't remember his name, but I was asked by Fliss. She should be here already." I watch as Callie looks around the house. We can hear a lot of noise out by the pool. I guess it's started already.

When we step onto the decking/patio area, my mouth drops even further. There are people everywhere. In the pool. At the side of the pool. There are a couple of sunbeds free so we grab them and put our bags and towels down. Callie is looking around for Fliss and then waves her over. I know Fliss; she's lovely. I think Callie has a crush on her, so I'm not too sure how today is going to go down.

"Hey, chick." Fliss hugs Callie.

"Hey. You remember Ainsley, right?" I know we've briefly met before.

"Yeah. Hi, Ainsley. How's things with you?"

"Great, thank you. Thanks for inviting us. This place is amazing."

"Yeah. C is great. He's a really busy guy, but he

likes to open up his house to parties once a month or so."

"Really? Is he not here himself?"

"No, not at the moment. He's working on a job, but he'll be here later." She smiles, takes our hands, and drags us over to the bar. "Right, ladies. What do you want to drink?"

There's a barman behind a very professional-looking bar, trying to do cocktails, and I laugh. No one is as good at cocktails as Hunter.

"Ladies, today we have an El Diablo cocktail as our house special."

"I'll have one of those please," I say, smiling at him. He smiles back at me and then winks. It feels good to have some male attention.

"I'll have one of those too," Callie says. She is talking to Fliss. They are both striking and I can feel the sexual chemistry from them both.

When we have our drinks, Fliss walks us around and introduces us to a few people. I don't remember their names; there are too many of them.

We are eventually back at the sun loungers and we sit on them and just take everything in.

After an hour or so, the party's in full swing and there are even more people here than there were earlier.

"I'm going to get in the pool," I say to Callie. "See you in a bit."

"See ya."

I take my sarong off and then jump into the pool. It's lovely in here and I swim up and down for a bit. I stop at the edge of the pool, lean up, and put my elbows on the side of the pool and just kick my feet behind me. It's so tranquil, even with the music blaring and everyone talking. I kind of lose myself in being relaxed.

There are some really hot guys, and one of them comes over to me.

"Hey, beautiful. Are you having fun?"

"Yeah. The pool is great."

He slips into the pool and leans up next to me. "What's your name? I haven't seen you here before."

"I'm Ainsley. What about you?"

He smiles. "I'm Marty." He holds his hand out for me to shake.

I laugh. "That's pretty formal considering we aren't wearing very many clothes," I say as I reach out and shake his hand.

He throws his head back and laughs. He's quite funny and keeps me entertained for a while.

When I get out of the pool, he swims off to the

other end and starts talking to another woman. I didn't give him any signals that I was single, so I didn't expect anything else from him.

"Fliss, I need to use the bathroom. Where is it?"

She smiles at me. "If you go back into the house and take the corridor on the right, it's the second door on the left."

"Thanks," I say, grabbing my towel and sarong.

Once again, when I'm inside the beautiful house, I can't help but admire it. Why would someone let people have a party in their house when they're not there? It doesn't make sense to me.

I take the right hand corridor. In front of me are six doors, three on the left and three on the right, and a staircase straight ahead of me. Shit. Which door did she say? Second on right or left? Or was it third on the left?

I open the third door on the left and hope it's the right one. Bollocks! It's not.

There's a guy inside and he's sitting at a desk with earphones on, and he's talking. It's like he's having a 'virtual' meeting.

"Look, I don't care what it takes. We need to close this deal. If we don't close today, then I'm out and they can find someone else to do it for them.

My price stands. No ifs, ands, buts, or maybes. Now go and sort it out. I'll be busy later, but send me a message and let me know if …" He turns around in his chair when he hears me open the door.

"Oops, sorry." I blush.

Oh my fucking God. He is gorgeous. He is tanned, with dark hair, slim build but with obvious muscles. He is wearing shorts and a t-shirt and his thighs are something to die for.

"Hold the line there a minute," he says into his microphone. "What are you doing in here?"

"I'm looking for the bathroom. I guess I got the wrong door," I say backing out of the room. "Sorry. Carry on."

"Wait!," he shouts as I close the door. I'm not hanging around to get into any more trouble.

I find the toilet next door and I dry myself off and then put my sarong on over my bikini. When I open the door to leave, he's standing on the other side of it. I scream.

He laughs. "Sorry. I didn't mean to frighten you."

"Well, you didn't do a good job of that, did you?" I say, laughing. "You nearly gave me a heart attack."

"Sorry. Are you having fun at the party?"

"Yeah. This house and grounds are so beautiful. How could you not enjoy looking at this all the time?"

He looks at me. "Yeah. Beautiful."

I blush.

Now I'm standing in the open bathroom door with this really handsome guy staring at me.

"Erm, I'd better go back to my friends," I say, trying to get past him.

He nods. Then he holds his hand out for me to shake. What is it with guys today? Can they not just say hi, my name is… and be done with it?

I take it.

"Let's start again. Hi, my name is C," he says, and I start giggling.

"I'm A. Pleased to meet you."

He smiles at me and I move past him. "I'll, erm, catch you later?" I ask.

"You sure will. If you get bored you can always come and help me out in here." He indicates his office.

"No, thanks. You sounded mean."

He laughs. "See you later, A."

"See ya." I turn and make my way back into the house.

Wow, he was intense, but, oh my God, he was

gorgeous. None of the other guys I've met today can hold a torch to him. He made my lady bits go all tingly and that hasn't happened for a while.

After taking a deep breath, I head back outside. Callie waves me over.

"Are you okay? You were gone a while. We were just going to come and look for you." She smiles and I notice how close she and Fliss are.

"I went through the wrong door. Instead of the bathroom, I found the office. And one hell of a gorgeous guy."

Fliss claps her hands. "Yay, you found C. He's beautiful, isn't he?"

"It's not really a word you'd use to describe a guy, but hell yeah, he sure is. I thought you said he was working on a job."

"Yeah. He does a lot of his work online, so he doesn't have to travel like he used to."

"Okay, that makes sense. He was shouting at someone to get the job done when I walked in."

"He might come out soon then, if he's been caught in the house."

"Hmm." My mind wanders to C. I'm distracted by a couple of guys who run and jump into the pool. As soon as they land, everyone else does the same.

"Come on, ladies! Let's go," Fliss says, taking Callie's hand and pulling her up. Callie does the same to me and the three of us run and jump into the pool.

Someone has set up the polo net and we play water polo. This is the most fun I've had in a long time. I'm really enjoying myself.

Our team loses and the penalty is that we have to down a few shots. I'm used to that at Mixology, so it's not that hard.

We climb out of the pool and towel dry before heading over to the cocktail guy.

"So, what shot do we have to drink then?"

"Sticky knickers," the barman says, winking at me.

"Really? Okay, hand one over then, big boy," I say, winking back.

Someone reaches out and puts their hand over mine. "If anyone's going to give her sticky knickers then it's me," he says, taking my shot and handing it to me.

"Oh my God. Did you really just use that line?" I ask, turning to look at him. I know who it is before I see his charming smile. The sun is behind him so I can't see his features properly, but I smile back at him.

"Yes, ma'am. I think I just did." He reaches out and takes a shot for himself. He clinks my glass. "To your sticky knickers." He smiles and downs the shot.

Laughing, I down mine too.

"Hey," I say. "You didn't play polo so you shouldn't have downed the shot!"

"It's my party, so I can do what I want," he says, moving closer to me.

"Is that right?" I stare at him. "What do you want to do right now?"

He stares me in the eyes and I can feel him looking deep inside me. He licks his lips and I swear he's going to kiss me. I gulp as he moves closer.

The next thing I know, he has lifted me in the air and is running for the pool.

"Fuck no. No way!" I scream as I thump him on the chest. He smiles at me and jumps up in the air and then we're both falling.

Before I get a chance to say anything else, we hit the water with a big splash. I laugh and swallow water as we fall down to the bottom. When I open my eyes, C is staring at me, smiling. I give him the finger, and when I touch the bottom of the pool, I push my feet off the bottom and come hurtling to the top. Gasping for breath, I hear everyone clapping as C comes up for air too.

"You bastard. I was dry and now... now I'm wet."

He laughs. "Glad I can make you wet so easily." He licks his lips once again.

I can't be mad at him; he's absolutely fucking gorgeous. His black hair is wet and slicked back so that I can see all his features. He moves towards me so I back up against the side of the pool.

"So, are you having fun?" he asks, trapping me by placing his hands on the wall behind me.

"Yeah. Seems you know how to throw a party." I smile.

"I like hearing people out here having fun. I live on my own and it doesn't matter how much I like this house, it gets lonely." His smile disappears slightly, but he quickly recovers.

"Yeah, I bet it doesn't get lonely with all these scantily clad women around here."

He leans in and whispers in my ear. "What women? I can't see any except for you."

I can't help but smile and my stomach does a backflip. Wow, what the hell? I blush. I just can't help myself. He's so handsome and he's being nice to me.

"Well, I see lots of good looking guys," I say, trying to look over his left shoulder.

"Are you sure?" he says, getting in my way.

"Yeah." I try to look over his right shoulder. His face moves again so I can't see anyone else. I laugh.

"Do you just see me now?" he asks, smiling. I look at him and the colour in his eyes changes. His pupils gets larger and he leans forward again. "I want to kiss you so bad right now."

My heart is racing so much. I've never wanted someone to kiss me as much as I want him to. I look around for Callie and I don't see her.

Fuck it. I make my own decisions.

I lean forward so my nose is almost touching his. "Do it." I open my eyes wide and lick my lips. He looks into my eyes and I feel like he's searching for something.

He looks at my lips, leans forward, and takes my tongue into his mouth. His hand drops from the wall to behind my neck and he brings me in closer. Our mouths move frantically, like we can't get enough of each other.

Our tongues are fighting for control and his other hand runs down to my lower back and he pulls me closer to him. Instinctively, I open my legs and wrap them around his waist. He backs me up against the wall and I can feel all of him against me. Fuck. He's huge.

When he pulls away, my lips are swollen, like they were assaulted - which they were.

"I can't move right now." He laughs. "But when I can, I think we should get out and have another shot. It will be time for me to barbecue then. Do you want to help me?"

I watch his eyes watching me. "I'd like that. I'd like to get to know you better."

He smiles at me. "I'd like that too."

A couple of hours later, everyone is sitting down and eating. C and I have cooked all the food and left it on the dining room table for everyone to help themselves. Callie and Fliss and a couple of the others have got everything else together. I've had so much fun. C is a great cook and so much fun to be around. I don't need to think about my brothers coming in and ruining it for me, so I relax and don't think about what will happen next.

After everyone has eaten, they all take their plates in and fill the dishwasher. I can tell they come here regularly because everyone seems so at home. C has disappeared into the house and Callie comes over to me. "Oh my God, Ains. He's gorgeous."

I smile at her. "Yes, he is. He's such a nice guy as well. I can't believe my luck."

She laughs. "Don't know how you're going to explain him to your brothers though."

"I'll worry about that when I have to. I've only known him a couple of hours. Who says he's going to want to see me after tonight?"

"I do." I hear him behind me. I turn and he looks at me and hands me a blanket. He walks away.

Callie laughs. "God, that was hot, and I don't even like guys," she says as she walks away. "Enjoy yourself and don't be good." She winks at me and heads off to find Fliss. I watch the two of them flirting and know I'm not the only one having fun.

I look for C and find him handing out blankets to everyone and then he puts some wood into the fire pit in the middle of where we're sitting. When he sits back down, he pulls me onto his lap.

"You look like you're having fun there." He kisses my neck. "I can't believe you came here today. It's like fate." He kisses along my shoulder.

"I bet you say that to all the girls." I laugh, but a clenching feeling in my stomach makes me stop. I bet he does this at every party.

"Actually, I don't usually stay so long. I normally

come out to cook the food and just chat to people and then I go back to work. I never have a reason to stay. Tonight is different. Tonight, I want to stay here with you wrapped around me all night. Go figure!"

I lean back into his chest. "I want to stay wrapped around you all night too," I say, looking into his eyes. He very slowly leans down and kisses me. When he pulls away, he whispers, "All night?"

I gulp. I know I said I want a shag, but am I ready for a one night stand? I slowly nod. "Yeah. All night."

He holds me tight. Ten minutes later, he stands and says, "Party's over, guys. I have an early start in the morning and need to get some beauty sleep." He turns around and winks at me.

Fuck, this is going to happen sooner than I thought. Callie and Fliss come over to me. "Are you coming with us? Or are you staying to help him with his beauty sleep?" Callie laughs.

Fliss leans over and whispers, "I heard he's an animal in bed."

"I'm staying," I say quickly, before I can change my mind. They both laugh and hug me.

"See you tomorrow, Ains. Can't wait to catch up."

They both walk away, taking others with them. I take a seat back down on the chair and wrap the blanket around me, staring into the flames that are dying down. This is so peaceful and so different to how my normal nights would be spent. I could get used to this.

"So, do you want to go inside or do you want to stay out here a bit longer?" he asks, taking my hand.

"Can we stay until the fire burns out?" I ask, nodding towards the fire pit.

"Of course. We can do whatever you like." He pulls me up and then sits back down, pulling me down on top of him. He wraps the blanket around me and we sit in silence for what feels like forever, just watching the flames.

"Why do you really have parties like this if you work when people are here?" I ask, curious to find out more about him.

He's quiet for a while. "I don't let people into my life easily. I lost my best friend when I was younger and I've never replaced him."

"Oh my God," I say, swivelling in the chair so I'm straddling him. I touch his face and he leans into my hand. "I'm so sorry to hear that." I kiss him on the lips very gently.

"He didn't die or anything, but something

happened that pulled us apart. I think about him all the time. I saw him recently, but he didn't know I was there." He looks so sad.

"You must have felt really strongly for him as a friend."

"Yeah I did. He thinks I betrayed him, but I didn't."

"Did you not tell him that?"

"Of course I did, but he was so pig-headed that he wouldn't listen. Anyway, I don't let people close because they can only hurt you." His whole demeanour changes. I feel him tense underneath me.

Leaning down, I kiss him and run my fingers through his hair, pulling him closer to me, hoping he forgets about his friend and thinks about me again. His hand runs all over my body, pulling me in closer to him. He moans and I feel him getting hard underneath me.

I grind down on top of him and he thrusts his hips up to get closer to me. He pulls away suddenly. "I need to take you inside or I'm going to fuck you here on this chair and you are too nice for that." He tried to push off the chair with me attached to him.

I push his chest so he sits back down on the chair. "I'm sick of being the nice one. I want to be the naughty one... the dirty one. What if I want you to fuck me on the chair? Would you refuse me?"

"No fucking way."

"Good. What if I want you to take me inside and fuck me everywhere after? Would you do that?"

"I like your thinking. I want to fuck you over every table, chair, and work surface there is, and finally, I want to make love to you in my bed. How does that work for you?"

I grin. "That works well for me. Now, shut up and let me fuck you on this chair."

He grins and then reaches down to take my bikini top off. Once he releases my tits, he's on them with his mouth, and when he takes my nipple in his mouth I'm gone. "Fuck, that feels good."

"You taste good," he says, and then he takes the second one into his mouth. His other hand is running down to my bikini bottoms. Luckily for him, they are tied at the sides, so all he has to do is loosen the bows. They slide down and he moans as he runs his hand down between my legs.

He runs his finger in between my lips before plunging one of them inside me. "Oh my God, that feels so fucking good."

"Not as good as it feels for me, baby." His mouth finds its way up to mine. His other hand is pulling my hair back so that my neck is exposed to him and he starts kissing my neck. They're not small pecks; they are big, hungry kisses. I'm probably going to be marked tomorrow, but I don't care. If this is all I get with him, one night, then I intend to make it worth my while.

I pull away slightly and climb off him. "Where're you going?" he asks with a twinkle in his eye.

"I am evening this out and taking your shorts off. I'm naked," I say, giving him a twirl, his eyes widening as I do. I kneel down in front of the chair and reach up for his shorts. He lifts his hips as I start to slide them down. His huge cock springs free. It's like a jack in the box when the lid opens. I smile to myself.

When his shorts are at his feet, I lean over and take his dick into my mouth.

"Fuck, that feels good," he says, thrusting into my mouth. Reaching out, I put my hand at the base of his cock and start fisting him as I take him deeper and deeper into my hot mouth.

He pulls my hair to make me stop. "You need to stop that or I'm going to be like a school boy on his virginal expedition." He laughs.

Climbing up onto the chair, I'm very aware that

we're both naked and that, when I sit down, I will be sitting on his cock. Lowering myself down, I make sure I don't take him inside. I need to tease him a little more before I fuck him. My lips are wet and they part to run up and down his cock as I move backwards and forwards.

"You tease," he says. "You know how bad I want to get inside your pussy? So fucking bad."

"I want you in there too, but first, I want to drive you wild." I lean over and kiss him. He devours me and lifts me slightly so his cock can stand to attention, then he lines me up and pushes me right down.

"Fuck," I shout into the dark night. "Oh my God, that is so fucking deep. Give me a minute." I lean into his chest. I can hear his heart beating and I'm sure it's going as quick as mine. Once I get used to his size, I lean over again and kiss him as I slowly move up and down his shaft. He moves his hands to my waist and as he destroys my mouth with his. He destroys my pussy with his cock. It's wild! It's amazing! It's everything I've ever wanted. I don't want men to treat me like I'm fragile. I won't break. I want to be treated rough. I want to be spanked. I want to have my hair pulled. I want... I want him to do all of that to me.

He must have read my mind because he pulls on my hair so I throw my head back. He kisses down my throat and even nips it. It makes me clench my pussy. He groans. I reach out and put my hands on his shoulders, and before he can stop me, I start fucking him with abandonment. I can see he's losing it; he wants me to come so he can come.

Leaning forward, he takes one of my nipples in his mouth, and when I have my head thrown back, he bites my nipple. I scream. I want to shout at him, but my pussy loved it so much, the orgasm is coming. He takes the other one in his mouth, and this time, I'm anticipating the bite. When it comes, it's bittersweet.

I want him to bite me more, but I want this orgasm and I want him to lose himself inside me. I lose my shit. I start orgasming like I've never orgasmed before. I scream into the dark night and he starts pumping so fast I fear the chair is going to break.

"Fuuuck!" He dumps his load inside me. He slows down and then I flop onto his chest. We are both breathing heavily and it takes time for us to be able to speak.

"That was fucking amazing." He runs his fingers through my hair.

"It certainly was," I say, nuzzling further into his chest.

He pulls my hair again so that I look up at him. "I need a drink before I can go again. Do you want one?"

I nod my head, too tired to talk. He lifts me off him and walks, butt naked, into the house and comes out moments later with a beer for me. He sits back down and pulls me on top of him and covers us with the blanket.

"Thanks," I whisper, and take a sip.

We sit in silence for a long time, neither of us wanting to break the quiet out here. We can hear the water in the pool trickling, and the logs burning and spitting out ash. But most of all, we can hear each other breathing. It's not an uncomfortable silence.

After we finish our beer, the fire is taking its last breath before the embers turn black, no longer emitting any heat. The blanket is not enough to keep us warm, and I start to shiver. He lifts me up, carries me inside the house, and places me on the worktop in the kitchen.

I look at him, confused, as he wraps the blanket around me and slides me to the edge. "Do you know how much I needed you to come into my life?"

"I've only just got here. You don't need me. You seem to be doing fine on your own."

"I needed someone who could see the real me hidden behind the façade of the cool guy who throws parties. You can see through that. I like that. You're a breath of fresh air."

I laugh. He makes me feel different to how I've ever felt before. He makes me want to be naughty and do things I've only heard of. It's like a primal, animalistic feeling.

He leans forward and kisses me, and I feel an emotion running through me that I haven't felt before. This is moving really fast. His hands are on my thighs and he is rubbing my legs. My eyes travel up and look straight in his, challenging him.

"I told you I want to fuck you on here. Do you have any objections?" he asks, raising an eyebrow.

"I have no objections. I want to see if you can live up to your promises!"

3 PINK PANTIES

*12 oz can frozen pink lemonade, 12 oz gin, ½ cup vanilla
ice cream, ½ cup frozen strawberries, 1 cup crushed ice*

The sun shining through the window wakes me and then I feel the heat of a man lying behind me. I haven't woken to a man in bed for a long time now. My brothers always see to that. I smile to myself, thinking how my brothers would react if they could have seen me last night.

"Are you laughing?" I hear a grumble behind me.

"Sorry," I say, rolling over so I can see his face. He is still gorgeous in the morning light. He smiles.

"I hope you weren't laughing at me."

"No, I certainly wasn't. I have to go soon." I

don't like the awkwardness the next morning. I make to move out of his bed.

He grabs me and rolls me back so I'm underneath him and he's hovering over the top of me. "Not so fast. I want to see you again. What do you think?"

My heart races so fast. I want. I want. "I'd like that," I say, trying to be calm. "What do you have in mind?"

"What about a trip out to sea? Do you like sailing?"

"I love sailing. It's the one time I can feel truly relaxed. Nothing can disturb you and ruin your day," I say, staring at his face. Reaching up, I run my hand along his cheek. He leans into my hand and then he kisses me. I push him off. "Urgh. Morning breath."

"Listen, baby, I kissed you after you sucked my cock. I don't think morning breath is going to put me off you." He laughs. He's right. I run my hand behind his head and bring his face closer to mine and kiss him like it's the last time. Who knows, with my brothers around, it might be.

"I don't think I got around to making love to you last night, so I can't leave you with broken promises," he says as he starts kissing down my chest to my belly button. Everything is different in the light of day and I squirm, thinking he can see me and what I look like naked. I don't think about the fact that I walked around his house last night naked for three or four hours.

An hour later, we get up and shower together; it feels so natural. I haven't ever felt as comfortable as I do with him. He throws me a t-shirt, and after putting it on, I follow him out to the kitchen. He lifts me up on the work surface where he fucked me last night and I blush, thinking of the memories.

He starts making breakfast. "Don't you have to go to work?" I ask him.

"I work for myself, mainly from home. I think you saw my office yesterday."

"What do you do?"

"Marketing. I've got some really big customers and it suits me to work here. I'm away for a lot of time when I have to travel abroad and it just makes life easier for me. What about you? What do you do?"

I gulp. "I just work in a bar. I love it, but I work most nights."

"A bar? Oh, which one? I must come and say hello when you're working," he says, and I blush. There is no way I can tell him where I work. My brothers would have a fit if this handsome guy came into Mixology looking for me.

"It's quite new. Anyway, that's enough about me." I reach out and grab him to kiss me. He leans his forehead on mine after the kiss.

"How did you come into my life when I least expected you?"

"I don't know what you mean."

"I'd given up on finding someone who I felt a connection with. But you… you give me hope."

"You're different to most guys. I don't know what it is, but I like it."

He pulls me into a hug and then makes me breakfast.

We sit chatting until about twelve and then he has to answer a call. I walk into the office after I'm dressed in my own clothes and interrupt his call.

"Yeah, hang on a minute," he says into the phone. "Are you running out on me?" he asks with a smile on his face.

"I have to go home to get ready for work. Thanks for last night." I smile at him and he pulls me into a hug and kisses my head.

"How will I get in touch to see you again?"

I kiss him on the cheek. "You're a man of many talents. You'll work it out," I say, turning and walking out of his office and his beautiful house.

I had already rung a taxi and it's waiting for me outside. After climbing in, I watch his house disappearing behind me and I lean back in the seat and close my eyes.

"We're here," the taxi driver says.

I open my eyes and pay him before climbing out and walking into my house. Like my brothers, I also live by the sea and have decking that sweeps around the house. As soon as I drop my bag, I walk out onto the decking and look across in the direction of C's house.

I can see his house from here. It's high up on the cliff, but I can just about make out his house and garden. I'll have to get myself some binoculars and then I can watch his parties. I shake my head and laugh to myself. God, I sound like a stalker. I go back into the house and change into some jeans and a t-shirt and then jump in my car and make my way down to Mixology to check in some orders and pay some bills.

Hunter is there when I arrive. "So, how was the

party? Did you enjoy your night off?" he asks as I head towards the office and get comfy.

"It was amazing. I had such a great night," I say, winking at Scarlett.

"You got laid, didn't you?" she whispers. I smile back and then Hunter walks in.

"You look like a girl who was naughty last night. What did you and Callie get up to? Can I ask questions? I'm intrigued."

I stand up. "Ewww. Oh my God! Really, Hunter?"

Scarlett laughs behind me. "You'll have to excuse this imbecile. He thinks it's really cool to see two women together and he wants to know the ins and outs. Just ignore him. He'll get over it."

"Sorry, sis. Just curious, you know." He leaves the office, and as soon as the door closes, Scarlett is on me.

She stands in front of my desk and leans down. "So... you got laid. Was it Callie?"

"What? No, Scarlett, it wasn't." I lean back in my chair and close my eyes. Memories are running through my head.

"Oh my God. You like him, don't you?" she says, sitting on the edge of the desk.

"It's complicated. I did get laid. Actually, I got

royally fucked. In fact, it was the best sex of my life."

"When are you seeing him again? I assume you're seeing him again."

"I didn't leave my number, but told him if he wanted to find me that much, then he would find a way."

"Romantic. What's his name?"

"That's the thing. I don't know his name. Everyone was calling him C, so that's what I called him. I even told him my name was A. He doesn't know who I am or where to find me."

What a stupid thing to do. Why did I do that? I could have easily given him my number, but I was caught up in the whole 'not knowing who he was' to think about it.

"What do you know about him?"

"His name begins with a C, he has a big house in Livermead overlooking the cliffs, he throws amazing parties, and he's in marketing."

"Okay. Well, it's up to him now. Just sit tight and wait."

My phone pings with a text. We both stare at it and my heart is racing so fast I can't breathe.

I look at it tentatively. "It's from Callie."

You had better have had a good seeing to last night for me to be woken at this time of day.

"What does she mean by that?" Scarlett asks.

"I haven't …."

My phone pings again.

I'm resourceful and I always get what I want. I want you on my boat tonight!

I read it out to Scarlet. "Fuck, fuck, fuck."

"What?"

"I can't go on his boat tonight. I'm working. I had last night off, so I can't be off tonight as well."

"Of course you can."

"No, I can't."

I'm working tonight, sorry. I can see you tomorrow during the day.

He doesn't reply straight away.

I feel like I'm holding my breath, waiting for him to reply, but it's only seconds.

I have a couple of meetings tomorrow. What about after work tonight? I can come and meet you.

"Shit. He wants to come and meet me from work tonight. What the fuck am I going to do?"

"Tell me again, what is the problem with you dating?" Scarlett asks with a smile on her face.

"You know the problem. My brothers would kill someone who was sleeping with me. They think I'm a virgin and they want me to stay that way for as long as I can. They want to hit anyone who comes within two feet of me and it drives me insane."

Scarlett starts laughing. I look at her and she stops. "Sorry, but it is funny. Do they think you live in medieval times or something? They don't have any say in your relationships. Do you want me to talk to Hunter and see if I can worm my way around him? I can just withhold a blow job or something. That usually works if I want something."

"Scarlett, that is way too much information."

We both start laughing.

I have to get back to C.

I'd rather you didn't. It's complicated. I can come to yours after work but it won't be until about two or three.

I'd take any time I can get with you. I'll see you later. C xx

We finish up within a couple of hours and then head home to rest until tonight. As I'm climbing into my car, I decide I'm going to call on C now. I don't want to wait until tonight.

I shoot him a text.

Are you around?

Always x

Are you home?

I am. Are you coming over?

Get the kettle on. I laugh to myself. I'm not going for coffee.

Kettle on. Clothes off. See you soon.

I drive up the hill towards his house and I can't help the butterflies in my stomach. I don't think I've ever been this excited to see a man who I'd only left a few hours before.

Pulling up outside his house, I take a couple of deep breaths to control myself. After climbing out of the car, I make my way to the front door, which is slightly ajar.

Pushing the door open, I close it behind me and walk into the kitchen. C is standing there, naked, making lunch. I laugh.

He turns and smiles at me. "Tea or coffee with your sandwiches?" he asks.

"Coffee, please. I didn't really expect you to make coffee, you know?"

"Oh, really? Did you think you could just come in here, fuck me, and leave? That's just plain taking advantage of me." He stalks over to me.

Laughing, I reply, "Hell yeah, I did."

He grabs hold of me and pushes me against the fridge. "Well, then let me do that before I feed you." He smiles and then takes my head between his hands and crashes his mouth down onto mine. He takes a breath. "I needed to feel your lips again. I was demented when you left and didn't leave me your number. Good job I remembered you were with Callie who knows Fliss. I had to go through the two of them before I could get to you. Now I don't intend to wait any longer."

He grabs my dress and pulls it up and then he picks me up. I wrap my legs around his waist and lean my head and neck back, arching as he pushes inside me in one quick motion.

"God, you're wet." He groans as he kisses my neck.

"Good job," I say, grinding down on his cock.

I hold on tight as he fucks me hard, not stopping until I have tears coming down my face from the emotion his fucking brings to me.

When we can breathe normally again, he slowly pulls out and lowers me to the ground. He kisses me one more time and then he turns back to finish making lunch.

"You'd better boil that kettle again. I think the

water has gone cold." I laugh. I feel really comfortable with C; more than I ever have before.

I walk over to him, lean against him, and wrap my arms around his waist from behind as he puts my sandwich on the plate.

His arse cheeks are rubbing my crotch and I loosen my grip to grab a hold of them and squeeze them.

"Ow," he says. "Did you just grab my arse?"

"Yes, I sure did," I say, laughing.

He turns around, picks me up over his shoulder, and spanks my arse. He then carries me over to sit on one of his kitchen stools and plonks me down. "Sit and keep your hands to yourself." He kisses me on the nose.

Laughing, he passes me a sandwich and a cup of coffee.

I take a bite of the sandwich; it's so tasty. Is there no end to his talents?

"You couldn't wait to see me later tonight then? Huh?" he says, smiling as he takes a bite of his sandwich.

"No. I decided I should just go for it. We could spend a lot of time just dancing around each other and waste time that could be spent fucking," I say, smiling back.

He laughs so loud I nearly fall off my chair.

"You are a breath of fresh air. I think you and I are going to get on really well."

"You think?" I ask, looking up at him.

"Oh yeah." It's quiet while we eat the rest of our sandwich and drink our coffee, and then he says, "So, do you still want to come on my boat tomorrow?"

"I'd love to. I like your company. I think we can have fun."

His eyes cloud over for a moment and then the darkness shifts. "Yeah, we sure can." He disappears down the hall, and when he comes back, he has shorts on.

"Come and sit outside with me." He reaches out to take my hand.

I follow him and then he sits in one of the sun loungers that had lots of bodies on last night. He pulls me down in front of him and leans back so that I'm resting against him.

He doesn't say anything. All I can hear is his breathing and the birds.

"I can see your house from mine. I stood on my balcony and thought about buying some binoculars, you know?"

He laughs and I can feel the rumble in his chest through my back.

"Stalker much?" He laughs.

"I know."

"What time do you have to be at work?"

I feel nervous talking about work. "About seven, but I have to go home and change first."

"Are you going to tell me where you work?"

"I don't want you coming there. The boss gets annoyed if the girls bring guys in. He says it affects their work and tips." It's true. Hunter would have a fit; that's if he got past Zac first.

"Okay, you'll tell me when you're ready." He kisses my cheek. "Are you coming back after work tonight?"

"You think I can just keep going and going? I need some sleep."

"I promise not to fuck you. We can just get cosy, talk, and sleep. Then, when we get up tomorrow, we can go on the boat and I'll have you back before your next shift. I promise."

Leaning back into him, I say, "Sounds like you have it all planned out."

"Yes, I do."

Two hours later, I'm showered, dressed, and standing at the door in Mixology. I can't help smiling. C makes me feel special and I think I deserve it.

Callie comes in and kisses me as she goes past. It's strange, but I feel guilty for kissing her. It's like I'm cheating on C. But I'm not really. Am I?

"Hey, Callie. Sounds like you all had a great time last night at the party," Zac says as she grabs my hand and tries to pull me into the bar.

"It was amazing. Can I just steal her for a few minutes? I won't be long, I promise." She winks at him and doesn't wait for an answer.

I follow her to the kitchen and she closes the door behind us. "You have to tell me what happened last night. Fliss went mad when C woke her up. Little did he know that we were together when he text." She laughs.

"So, you had a great night too?"

"I sure did. Best night of my life."

"I know that feeling," I say, smiling.

She grabs my hands and starts jumping up and down in the same spot. "Oh my God, you got laid. You got laid."

"Shh! I don't want my brothers hearing."

"Are you going to see him again?"

"Already have," I say, smiling so wide I think I'm going to split my face open.

"What? When?"

I laugh. "I went up there for lunch before I came to work this evening."

"Tell me, is he great in bed?"

"Well, we weren't really in bed much. But he's great on the lounger outside, fantastic on the kitchen counter..."

"Stop. Don't tell me anymore. I don't think I want to hear it. Do you want to hear about Fliss and me?"

"Not really. No offence."

She laughs. "I'm just so happy for you. Just be careful. Don't let him break your heart."

"I won't. I promise," I say, but know I'm already falling for C in a big way.

We go back to the front door and Callie heads into Mixology for a couple of drinks while I work. It's relatively busy. There's no trouble so it's a great night.

Callie comes out when she's going to leave. She comes up to me and kisses me on the lips. It feels weird and wrong.

"I'm going home," she says. "I'm meeting Fliss," she whispers in my ear.

"Okay, babe. I'll chat to you later."

She hugs me tight. "Love you."

"Love you."

When she leaves, Zac says, "I love the two of you together. You both look so happy. I'm glad you found someone to love, Ains. I know we aren't the easiest to be around. We love you and just want to protect you from arseholes."

"I know, Zac. Thanks. Do you think Hunter will mind if I sneak off early tonight? I want to go see her after work."

"Of course he won't mind. You work too much anyway."

I finish up about twelve and I text C.

I finished early. Are you home?

I'm at home and I'm waiting for you x

See you in a few minutes x

It only takes me about ten minutes to get to his house, and when I walk up his drive, he's waiting at the door for me. As soon as I step up to him, he grabs me around the waist, pulls me in close, and kisses me.

When he breaks free, I pant like a wild dog. "Did you miss me that much?" I ask, laughing as we walk into the house.

"I sure did. You, young lady, are distracting me

from my work. I can't seem to concentrate. All I can think about is you."

"I didn't know my pussy was that addictive." I laugh.

"It is. But I like you as a person too. You're funny and you push me and don't do everything that I ask you to. I love that. I love a challenge and you are a challenge."

"Is that the only thing you like about me? My being a challenge?"

"Oh God, no. I like the whole package. Especially when it's all wrapped up in me." He grabs my hand. "Come on. Let's go for a swim. It's still warm."

When we get outside, he takes his shorts off and jumps into the pool. The way he ran and jumped stirs something in me. I don't think it's a memory as such, but a feeling, and I don't know what it is. I shake my head, take off my clothes, and run and jump in on top of him.

We mess around in the pool for a while, and as I'm trying to get out, he pulls me back down into the water. "I know I said I wasn't going to fuck you tonight, but you're early and you look so gorgeous wet." He pushes my hair back off my face and stares at me. I didn't even realise he was pushing me backwards into the wall until I feel the cold at my back.

"I'm so glad you said that because I was thinking of ways to take advantage of you."

"Were you really?" he asks, smiling.

"Hell yes, I was. I need your cock in me as much as possible," I say with a straight face. He looks at me and then he laughs and I join in with him.

He kisses me and then grabs hold of my waist so I straddle him like I did last night, except tonight, we don't have any clothes between us.

His cock pushes at my entrance, and with a swift movement, he slams it inside. "C! Fuck, that's deep!"

I try to pull my head back but the wall is in the way so I lean it forward onto his shoulder. As he fucks me hard, I open my mouth and bite his shoulder.

"Ow," he shouts, but it doesn't stop his assault on my pussy.

"C, that feels so good. Don't stop. Please don't stop."

"I'm not stopping until your legs are so wobbly you can't stand and I'm going to have to carry you to bed."

"Don't over promise and under achieve," I say deadpan.

Again, he laughs. "God, you're amazing," he says as he speeds up.

"C, I'm coming. I can't help it. I don't know what button you're pressing, but keep pressing it. This one is coming all the way from my toes."

"I'm right behind you, baby. Right behind you."

I lose control and come everywhere. It makes me shake and shiver until I'm finished. I think I squeezed his cock so hard it could have snapped. He comes right after me. Then he leans over me, hugging me until we can both breathe again.

When we pull apart, he lifts me out of the pool and carries me into the bathroom. He places me on the seat and turns on the shower. When the heat is a good temperature, he lifts me again and puts me under the spray. As the water comes down over both of us, he hugs me tight and says, "I think you're here to save me. I'm so lucky." He kisses the top of my head and holds me.

When we've both warmed up, he turns the shower off, grabs a towel, and wraps it around me. He wraps one around himself too and then he dries me off. When I'm dry, he carries me into his bed and then dries himself before climbing in next to me. Neither of us says a word. It's a little bit over-whelming for me and I start to cry.

"What's the matter?" he asks, wiping my tears but not letting me go.

"Sorry. I'm being a real girl and that is so not like me."

"It's okay. Why are you crying?"

I take a deep breath. "I've never been looked after as much as you've looked after me in the last twenty-four hours."

"I don't understand. I've not really done anything," he says as he caresses my face.

"See, even now you're touching me and making sure I'm okay. No guy has ever done that. I've always been someone they want because of my family. They want a fuck and then they leave. That's life. You're different. I get the feeling you want to know me for me and not who I am."

"Who are you?" he asks as he pushes a strand of hair behind my ear.

"It's not important. I enjoy you not knowing. It means that you want to be with me." I smile at him.

"I do. I don't date much, and like I said, I don't spend time at the parties. I don't trust people, espe-cially women, and I don't get attached because I don't want to get hurt."

"That's a really girly thing to say." I laugh.

"I know. You make me feel things I've not felt before. I like you a lot. I can see you're hiding something and I want to know what it is, but I want to know you regardless." We lay in silence for a while then he asks, "Do you want any food or a drink?"

"No. I just want to lay here with you. Is that okay?"

"Baby, that is more than okay. That's what I want too."

CHOCOLATE BOOBIE

1/2 oz Jagermeister herbal liqueur, 1 oz Kahlua coffee liqueur, 1 1/2 oz milk

C

My alarm rings and I turn it off quickly, not wanting to wake her up. I lie looking at her. She's gorgeous and I can't believe she wants to be in my bed. I know I'm good-looking and can have my pick of women, but to be honest, she is the first woman I've looked at in a long time. I climb out of bed, put on my boxers, and then go into the kitchen to put the coffee machine on. While I'm waiting for it to brew, I stand, leaning against the counter, thanking my lucky stars that this amazing woman came into my house the other night.

I make the coffee and then make my way back down to the bedroom. When I open the door, I smile. She has rolled over in the bed and is like a starfish, taking up all the room. She looks great in my bed. It won't be the same without her in it again.

Putting her coffee on the bedside table, I gently wake her. "Hey, A. I've got to do a conference call and then we can head off to the boat. There's a coffee there. Just take your time." I kiss her on the head. She moans and rolls over to face me.

"Hey," she says, smiling at me. God, if I thought she was beautiful last night, I was wrong. She looks sexy with her mussed up hair, under my duvet, and looking at me with those big, beautiful eyes. She has tattoos, and I promise myself that I'm going to lick each and every one of them and find out if they have a story behind them.

"Hey," I reply when I can string a few words together. "I have to go take a call. I won't be long. Take your time." I lean down and kiss her before walking out of the bedroom.

In my office, I need to pull myself together and concentrate on the job in front of me and not the woman in my bed. My company is my world. I've worked hard at it since I left university and moved home. I have customers all over the world and regularly travel to see them. Most of my work is carried out over the computer. Thank God for Skype and video calls.

I've got my files out and I'm just getting set up when the video call light flashes on my computer. I've put a top on so that I look professional, but there's no shirt and tie for me. "Good morning, Johnson," I say to my client.

"Good morning, Ross."

"Let's get straight down to business. Tell me about your new product."

I take notes as he tells me all about a new product he wants me to market and get trade patents for.

An hour later, the door quietly opens and I see A standing there, looking at me. She has one of my t-shirts on and she looks gorgeous. I smile at her and then whisper, "Nearly done."

She nods, and as Johnson is talking to me about something really boring, she slowly lifts up the corner of my t-shirt. My eyes open wide.

"Ross, are you there? I can see you but what's going on your end?"

I turn to face him and smile. "Sorry. Something disturbed me and reminded me that I have another meeting to go to. How about you wind it up with some bullet points. I've taken notes, so send me through the draft patent details and I will get back to you later today."

I turn again and she's leaning against the door with her finger in her mouth, and the other hand is slowly pulling the t-shirt up just enough for me to see that she has no knickers on.

I open my eyes wide at her as I wrap up the call. She looks at the door. I know she's going to run as soon as I take the headset off and stand up. My shorts have tented with my large cock and she has pulled the t-shirt off completely and started running down the hall.

Running after her, I catch her, and she can't stop laughing.

"Find that funny, do you?" I ask as I grab her.

"I do," she says, laughing uncontrollably. "You should have seen your face. You couldn't keep your eyes off me."

"Did you expect me to?"

"No. I like your eyes on me." She looks shy again. I love the way she changes from hot to shy in one second flat.

"Now, what am I going to do with this?" I ask, pointing down to my cock.

She smiles at me and slowly lowers herself, looking at me the whole time, until she's facing my cock. Her small hand reaches out and grabs it and starts pumping it. I moan. Fuck, she is driving me wild. She moves it closer to her mouth and I hold my breath. Then she takes it into her mouth and runs her tongue around the end.

"Fuck." I tilt my head back to look at the ceiling. It feels so good.

She moans around my cock and then I feel the back of her throat. It's softer than the rest of her mouth. Her hand is at the base of my cock and her other hand is cupping my balls. I'm on sensation overload here.

"So. Good," I say, looking down at her as she looks up at me. The corners of her lips turn upwards in a smile.

She then tilts her head and takes me deeper. She pushes me back and then pulls me forward, telling me that she wants me to fuck her mouth.

Where the fuck did she come from? Why haven't I met her before?

"Baby, I'm going to come. I'm not going to be able to stop it."

She responds my pushing me in deeper and then she moans. The vibrations send me over the top and I blow my load all the way down her throat.

"Shit!" I shout. It feels like I've got enough cum to drown her.

When I'm still and my cock has stopped pulsating, I pull it out of her mouth. She grabs it at the last minute and licks it clean. No one has ever done that to me before. It's hot.

She looks up at me. "Was that sorry enough for you?" she says as she stands up and wipes her mouth with the back of her hand.

I laugh at her. Does she really think I need to answer that?

"You are one amazing woman. Come on. We'd better get dressed or we won't make it out of here today." I grab her hand and pull her down to the bedroom to get dressed.

Twenty minutes later, we're sitting in my car on our way down to the harbour. I'm looking forward to showing her my boat and taking off for the day. After parking my car, we walk out to the docking bays.

I can tell she's been here before. She knows where she's going and she keeps walking when I stop at my boat. It's a natural instinct, because she obviously comes here regularly.

"Hey, this is mine," I say, and she stops and turns back to me.

"Sorry," she says as she walks back to me.

"I take it you've got a boat as well?"

"Yeah. My dad has one over there." She points in the general direction she was walking.

I help her up onto my boat and she helps with organizing everything as I undo the ropes and put the bolsters out. She sits next to me as I get comfortable and turn the boat on.

"Let's hit the high seas and have some fun," I say as I guide us out through the harbour walls. "Which one is your boat?" I ask her.

"See that one over there?" She points. "The Verity."

Fuck. It had to be that boat. It could have been any other boat in the harbour, but no. It had to be that one.

I want to turn around and go home. I know today is not going to go well at all.

"Do you know the one I mean?" she asks, smiling at me.

"Yeah, I've seen it a few times."

I can't tell her I've been on that boat more than

once. She's obviously hiding who she is. Does that mean she knows who I am?

Once we've gone past them, I push the throttle and we move faster out to sea.

I glance over at her and she's sitting next to me with her hair flying in the wind, looking gorgeous, and I take a picture of her in my mind because this might be the last day I get to spend with her.

"Do you want to go to Dartmouth? We can either dock and go for lunch in the town or on the floating restaurant. Your choice," I say, smiling at her.

"Let's go into the town. We can grab some food and then walk down to the castle. It's lovely there."

"Great idea." I lean over and kiss her. Today might be the last day I get to take her out. When she knows who I am, things *will* change.

I steer us to Dartmouth and we dock at the open marina.

Once we've secured the boat, I take her hand and help her off the boat, then we head to a little kiosk that sells freshly made crab sandwiches. When we have everything we need, I grab a bottle of wine and we walk down to the castle. It's a small castle, but it's at the end of the bay and you can see the entrance to the River Dart and the open sea. I used to love coming here as a child and it brings back loads of memories.

Sitting down, I hand her her sandwich and open the bottle of wine. "Do you mind drinking out of the bottle?" I laugh. "We can pretend we're teenagers drinking without our parent's permission."

She shakes her head. "I don't mind." She takes the bottle and takes a big swig. I do the same.

"You've gone quiet. What's up?" she asks.

"Nothing."

"Don't lie to me. You've not been the same since we got on the boat. Did I say something to upset you?" When she looks at me, I see her eyes are glazed over. I didn't want to talk about this now, but she's not going to stop until she knows what's changed.

I take a deep breath. "Your name is Ainsley, isn't it?"

Her eyes open wide. "How do you know that?"

"Just a guess."

"Is that a problem? Knowing my name?"

"No. It's just I have to tell you something and I know you're going to hate me after."

She sits upright. "Just tell me. Everything will be fine."

"My name is Cooper." I don't say any more. I don't need to.

"Cooper? As in Hunter's best friend?"

I nod.

She jumps up. "Fuck!" Then she starts to cry.

I can't watch her crying so I jump up and take her in my arms and try to hug her. She tries to pull away, but I don't let her go. If I do, she won't listen to me.

"Stop! Let go of me. I want to go home."

"Ainsley, listen to me. I'm sorry. I didn't know who you were until you told me about your dad's boat. I've been on that boat so many times. I want to explain to you what happened at university. I need you to listen to me though. Hunter never did. Please?"

I hold her tight. I don't want to let her go. I need her to listen to me. She stops hitting me and seems to calm down. "Let's sit down. Please, Ainsley? I like you a lot. I remember when I used to come around to visit and you would be there; you were such a brat. I'm surprised I didn't recognise you, but it has been a long time. You were busy playing with your dolls when I used to come over. I work abroad a lot of the time and don't really do the whole society scene."

She sobs. "Maybe that's why we get on so well." At least she recognizes our feelings. "Hunter made us take down any pictures of you when he came home from Australia so I haven't seen them for years."

I let her go and she looks up at me with sadness in her eyes. This is a lot for her to take in. Abruptly, she sits down and grabs the bottle of wine and takes a big swig. She hands it to me and I take some before sitting down with her. Grabbing her, I move her in front of me so my body is wrapped around hers.

"Talk," she says.

Taking a deep breath, I begin. "You know Hunter and I were best friends since primary school? We did everything together and when we got into the same university, it was the best feeling ever. Grace was a bitch, but he couldn't see it."

"So you wanted to show him how much of a bitch she was? Is that what you're saying." She takes another drink.

"Ainsley, please. Let me finish. She kept trying it on with me and told me that she didn't love Hunter, but that because he was so popular she got to go to parties that she wouldn't have been invited to if she wasn't with him."

"Bitch."

"Yeah, she was. That night, I had gone to their room to see Hunter and tell him she had tried it on with someone at the party. When I got there, she was naked on the bed. Her eyes lit up when she saw it was me and she was trying to pull me down onto the bed. I was fully clothed when Hunter walked in. I was telling her no! I told her I was going to tell him what a bitch she was and she must have seen him coming in because she pulled me down to her and tried to kiss me."

I take a swig of wine and pass it back to her.

"He lost the plot. Kicked us both out and wouldn't take any of my calls or messages. The next thing I knew, he had disappeared. I tried to talk to Keaton and Zac, but they wouldn't entertain me. The James family are tight, you know." I laugh.

"Too right we are."

"I promise you, nothing ever happened with me and Grace and it was never going to. I was really hurt when he wouldn't speak to me and I've never let any friends close since."

"He's the best friend you were talking about, isn't he?" she whispers.

"Yes, he is. When I moved back, I thought I would see him around town, but then I heard he had moved to Australia. I was shocked. By the time he moved home and opened Mixology, too many years had passed for me to explain myself."

"You could have tried."

"He would have kicked me out of the bar. Zac would have taken great pleasure in kicking my arse."

She laughs. "That is so true."

We sit there for a while, not speaking. "This is going to be difficult, isn't it?"

"It doesn't have to be. I want to see you. I think we have something special and I want to give us a chance. But I know how difficult it's going to be for you."

"Argh! I want to see you too. I just know how Hunter will take it."

"You know I saw him recently. Remember I told you I lost a friend and had seen him?"

"Did you? Did he see you?"

"Not really. I looked after him and called the ambulance for him when he was attacked. I talked to him, but he didn't recognise me he was so badly beaten. I rang the hospital to check up on him though."

"That was you?" She turns in my lap. "Thank you so much. He could have died." She reaches her hand out to touch my face and kisses me. "Thank you."

My heart speeds up. Maybe we can make this work. I know I really want to. "He would have done it for me, regardless of what he thinks happened with Grace. I know he would."

"I'm not so sure about that." She laughs. "Let's see how our relationship develops. You might get bored with me in a week." She smiles at me.

"I doubt it. I've never had so many feelings so quickly with a woman as I have with you, and do you know what? It doesn't scare me. But Hunter scares me. The James family scares me. They are the ones that can tear us apart."

"I won't let them, Cooper." She runs her hands through my hair and starts pulling it. "This is how you make me feel. You make me want to strip naked and fuck you right here. Even after telling me what happened."

I tilt my head to look her in the eye as she pulls my hair. She's grinding on my lap and my cock is really hard.

"God, Ainsley, I want you so bad." I put my hands behind her neck and pull her close. I take her bottom lip in mine and she moans as I nip it gently. I plunge my tongue inside her mouth and we're both lost in the feelings we have. She grinds down on my cock and there is nothing I want more than to climb inside her. There are people walking around us, and some are tutting, but I don't care. I want this woman more than I've wanted anything in my life.

The situation with Hunter should make me run for the hills, but I can't. I don't want to leave her and never know what could have happened between us.

We eventually pull apart. I kiss her on the lips briefly and then I whisper in her ear, "Let's get back on the boat. I want to fuck you in the middle of the ocean."

Her eyes open wide. "I want that too, Cooper." My name on her lips turns me on so much.

She climbs off my lap and holds her hand out to me, offering to help me up, but there is no chance I can go anywhere with this hard on. "Baby, I need to wait a few minutes. Let's finish the sandwiches and then we can go back."

She looks down at my cock and laughs. We finish our sandwiches and then walk back to the boat. After leaving the estuary, I head out further into the ocean.

"I know this is going to be difficult and I know

you don't want to tell your family about me yet. I understand that. But I know that I want to be with you, Ainsley, so at some stage, you are going to have to tell them."

"I know I am. Just let's enjoy some time together first. Please?"

Cutting the engine on the boat, I stalk my way over to her. "Any way in particular you want to enjoy our time right now?"

She smiles and opens her legs. She is going to be the death of me.

~

AINSLEY

Oh my God, Cooper rocks my world. He understands me and I love spending time with him. I just can't believe he's Cooper. The Cooper that Hunter thinks stole his girlfriend. If our relationship lasts, which I hope it does, this is going to cause real problems.

After he fucked me into oblivion, we eventually dock back in the harbour. I help him moor the boat and then we close everything up. He grabs my hand and we walk to his car and drive back to his house.

As we pull up in his drive, my phone beeps with a text. It's Hunter.

Dinner's nearly ready. Where are you?

Shit!

"Cooper, I have to go. I forgot we have a family dinner today. I'm sorry. I had a great day," I say, leaning over and kissing him.

"No problem. Will I see you later?"

"Are you sure you don't want a break from me yet?"

"I know I don't."

"Then I'll be over when I finish work. Leave the door open if you go to bed."

"I'll be awake." He kisses me with so much passion I want to cry.

Getting out of the car is the hardest thing I've done. I want to give up work and spend all my time with him. It's insane.

"I'll see you later," I say, walking back to my car.

Fifteen minutes later, I run into Mum and Dad's shouting, "I'm home!"

When I walk into the lounge, Hunter stares at me. Shit, does he know?

"Sorry I'm late. I went out for lunch with Callie and I didn't realise the time." Everyone relaxes and I help Mum bring the food out.

"So, you've been busy the last few days. What have you been up to?" Mum asks me.

"Not much. I went to a fantastic party the other night with Callie. We had a really good time." I hope I'm not blushing.

"That's good. I like Callie. She has a good head on her shoulders," Mum says, smiling at me.

"Yeah. She keeps me grounded."

Everyone talks about what they've been doing and I tune out. I wish I could tell them about Cooper. I can't stop thinking about him and how happy he makes me. Scarlett leans over and whispers in my ear, "Out for lunch with Callie my arse! You got well and truly fucked, didn't you?" She laughs.

I whip my head towards her. I can't lie; I know it's written all over my face. I simply nod. We both laugh.

Zac is talking about what he and Issy have been up to and they all look at us laughing.

"Sorry," I say. 'Scarlett just told me a joke."

Zac looks annoyed but I don't care. I'm happy.

ADIOS MOTHERF*#CKER

½ oz vodka, ½ oz rum, ½ oz tequila, ½ oz gin, ½ oz Blue Curacao liqueur, 2oz sweet & sour mix, 2oz lemonade soft drink

TWO WEEKS LATER

Life has been amazing. I've spent every single night at Cooper's since I met him. I'm hardly at my house, only to get more clothes. We have so much in common and I crave him when I'm at work. He works while I work so the rest of the time we get to spend together.

I'm just getting ready for dinner as I have the night off and Cooper is going away on business tomorrow for a week. I don't know how I'm going to cope back in my own house, without him.

"Dinner's ready," he shouts from the kitchen. We aren't going out because of my family. I don't want to bump into someone who will tell Hunter. Not yet, anyway.

Walking into the kitchen, I move up behind him and hug him. He has a pair of black slacks on, and a white shirt, which is open at the neck. He looks gorgeous. I have a beautiful red dress on that clings to my body.

"Mmm, I like it when you hug me like that." He slowly turns in my arms and kisses me. "We need to sit down or we won't get any food."

I reluctantly pull away from him and help to carry stuff over to the table.

Dinner is amazing. I'm so lucky; he's a great cook. We take it in turns to cook but we never do anything formal like this.

After we've eaten, he says, "I can't believe I'm leaving you behind tomorrow. You could come with me."

I laugh. "I know, but I can't get time off work yet. Anyway, we can video chat. I hear sexting is fun these days."

He laughs out loud. "Oh, I can't wait to do that."

"Seriously though, Coop, I'm going to miss you so much."

"I know, Ains. Me too. I wanted to talk to you about something, I know it might be difficult, but I really want you to think about it while I'm gone."

"What?"

"I want you to move in with me." He holds his hand up because he knows I'm going to protest. "I know it's soon, but you've spent every night here and I don't want to think of you in your bed on your own. I know there are a lot of obstacles in our way, but we need to face them head on or we won't ever get past the sneaking around stage. I'm not fifteen anymore and I don't want to sneak around with you. I want to show you off and tell everyone you're mine."

I want to cry. He says the sweetest things, but it's also the hardest thing for me to do. "I know I have to tell everyone. I don't want to sneak around either. I'm just worried that my life is going to change so much when I tell Hunter."

"I'm not asking you to choose. I'd never ask you to do that. I want to be the one to tell him and set him straight about what happened, but I know that's not how you want things to go either. I'm leaving this one in your court, but when I come back, we need to talk about how we move our relationship forward."

"I know what I need to do. I just don't know how to do it. What if I tell him and he hates me? What will I do then? What if you dump me when you come back and my brother hates me?"

He gets off his chair and comes around to my side of the table. "Ainsley, I'm not going to dump you. You're it for me. I feel like we were destined to be together. I've always liked you and you feel like I'm coming home."

I start to cry. He's so sweet. He pulls me off the chair and carries me over to the couch and sits me down on his lap. "Baby, I know this is probably the hardest thing you have ever had to do and I wish I could do it for you. I want you to move in with me when I get back. I've never felt this way before. You're my forever, babe."

I lean into him and sob. No one has ever been so nice to me before. I feel like a vulnerable child. This is something that could change the dynamics of my family and that breaks my heart.

We leave the dishes and he carries me to bed. After taking my clothes off, he removes his too. I feel like a rag doll as he moves the duvet so I can climb into the bed. He leans over me and kisses me gently. I love his kisses. They set off feelings in me I never knew I had. My heart races, the butterflies in my stomach go wild, and I just want to lose myself in him.

One of his hands runs down my body and then he moves down. He kisses my nipples on this way and then kisses down my stomach to my pussy. Naturally, my legs open, and he looks up at me. He pulls my lips open and licks his tongue between them. I arch my back. It feels so good when he touches me there. He slowly inserts one finger, then a second and he fucks me with his fingers. I moan as I arch backwards and I pull his hair and push his head back down.

He twists his fingers inside me and they hit the spot that sends me wild. I start shouting his name as my orgasm takes over my body. Slowing down his assault on my pussy, he pulls his fingers out. He watches me while he licks them clean.

Slowly, he moves back up my body until his cock is at my entrance and then as slowly as he has been doing everything else, he pushes himself inside, inch by perfect inch.

This is the slowest and most beautiful sex we've

ever had, and I want to cry. It feels like he's saying goodbye.

As he thrusts inside, he pulls my legs up and pushes them back so that he gets deeper. He leans down and kisses me and we become one person, moving together.

He lets go of my legs, leans down on top of me, and kisses me as he thrusts in and out. "Come, baby. Come. I can't hold on much longer. I want to feel you come over my cock."

His dirty talk sets me off and I feel the sensation in my toes as it creeps up my body and starts to make me shake. "Fuck!" I shout as my orgasm rips through me. He follows me seconds later and then drops on top of me.

When his breathing becomes more stable, he looks up at me and says, "I love you, Ainsley. I hope you know that."

Tears well up in my eyes. Jesus, he's making me a cry baby.

I'm getting ready for work in my own house; something I haven't done for a couple of weeks. It feels strange. I feel lost. Cooper text me when he landed and we've been texting back and forth since. It's not the same though, but things have got kind of serious very quickly between us.

When I'm dressed, I head down to Mixology with a heavy heart. I know what I need to do. I'm just too chicken shit to do anything about it.

"Hey, Ains," Hunter says as I let myself in the front door. "You okay? You seem different these days. We don't see much of you outside Mixology."

"I'm fine. Just been busy, that's all." I say as I walk past the bar and into the office. Scarlett is there already.

"Hey, boss," she says. I laugh. I really like her; she's like the sister I never had.

"Hey yourself. What have you been up to?" I ask her.

"Not much. Hunter is trying to work out how we can all go to Australia to see Keaton and Dakota in their tournament."

"Someone needs to stay here and run Mixology. I don't mind doing that," I offer, knowing I wouldn't be able to bring Cooper with me, even if I wanted to.

"No way. You need a holiday as much as Hunter does. It's all of us or no-one. That's what he says."

"Cool," I say, not really meaning it.

She rolls her chair over to my desk. "Are you okay, Ainsley? You've been very reserved recently. Did you and that guy split up or something?"

"No. That's part of the problem, to be honest. I don't want to introduce him to the boys. They might ruin what we have."

"They love you, babe. They just want you to be happy. They don't want a time-waster breaking your heart, that's all."

I smile at her. Cooper is not a time-waster at all. Little does Hunter know, but he will be breaking my heart soon when he finds out.

I'm back out at the door with my cup of coffee and one for Zac. A couple of hours later, when Callie comes in, I feel really bad because she still kisses me and hugs me when and I feel like I'm cheating on Cooper. I told her who he is and she knows what I'm going through.

My phone pings with a text while she's beside me and I can't hold myself back from answering it.

It's Cooper, of course.

Hey baby, miss you already.

Miss you too xx

Are you working right now?

Yeah, I'm here with Callie and Zac. Watching the door

I want to send you something. Make sure no one looks at your phone

Ooh can't wait

I quickly hide my phone.

It takes a couple of minutes for my phone to beep again, and when I look at the picture he sent me, I know I'm blushing. He sent me a picture of his hard cock in his hand.

This is what happens when I think of you baby. .

"Who's that you're talking to, Ains? You're blushing," Zac says, walking towards me and reaching out to take my phone.

"Fuck off, Zac. That's my phone and my business," I say, putting the phone in my pocket.

"Just curious as Callie is right beside you!"

"Just leave me alone. I'm sick of this family dictating what I can and can't do in my life," I say, before storming into the bar and through to the office. I slam the door behind me and start to cry. Why did I have to fall in love with the one man my family hate?

There's a quiet knock on the door. "Ainsley, it's Issy. Can I come in?"

I move out of the way and open the door. She walks through, sees me crying, and comes over to hug me. "Come on, Ains. This isn't like you. You're the glue that holds everyone together."

"No, I'm not!" I sniffle into her shoulder.

"Yes, you are. The boys love you and respect you so much. Zac was so worried out there that he left the front door to come and find me to ask me to check on you. He never leaves that door unless you're there. You know that."

"I'm sorry. There's just some stuff going on I can't talk about."

Scarlett comes in and hugs me too. "You know we're here for you, don't you?"

"I know. But your priority is to the boys and I don't want to put you in an awkward position."

"Okay, understood," Issy says. "How about we have a girly day later this week and go for cocktails and some shopping? I'm sure the boys will manage without us for the day."

Scarlett nods and says, "I think that's a great idea. You in, Ains?"

"Yeah, I'd like that a lot. I think I might go home now though. I need some time on my own."

"I'll cover the door with, Zac," Issy says. "He won't like it, but he can lump it." She smiles, kisses me on the cheek, and then leaves.

"Is this about your mystery guy?" Scarlett asks.

"Yeah. I don't want him to be a mystery though. I want my family to know him like I do."

"So what's the problem with that? Just tell them. They'll be happy for you."

"I can't, Scarlett. I'll tell you more when I can, but right now, I can't talk about it."

There's another knock at the door and Hunter comes in. He takes one look at me and pulls me into a hug. "Hey sis. What's the matter? You're never sad."

"I don't think I can work tonight. Do you mind if I go home?"

"Of course not. Do you want Scarlett to go with you? Or will you be all right on your own?"

"I might go and see Mum and Dad."

"Okay, that might be a good idea." He hugs me tight.

When he lets go, I say goodbye and walk out of the door. I hear Hunter say to Scarlett, "I'm worried about her. She's not herself these days."

"She'll tell you what's wrong when she's ready. Give her time, Hunter."

As soon as I get in the car, I ring Mum. When she answers, I say, "Mum, can I come over and stay the night?"

"Of course you can. Your bed is always made. You know that."

"Thanks. See you in ten minutes."

I drive over to their house. I'm going to tell her what's going on. She'll tell me what to do for the best.

".... So now I'm in a situation, Mum. I've fallen in love with a man my family hate and I don't know what to do about it. He told me his side of the story and what he did for Hunter when he found him beaten up on the ground. That doesn't sound like someone who did what Hunter thinks he did."

Mum and Dad have listened to me talk for the last twenty minutes about Cooper. I told them I didn't know who he was and how we fell for each other before we found out.

"Ainsley, from what I know of Cooper, he is a wonderful man. He was always like a son to us, and when Hunter left England, we blamed him for it. From what you've just told us, I believe you, because Grace was never nice when she was here. You need to tell Hunter before he finds out from someone else. He will be devastated if you don't tell him.

Explain to him the way you just did to us and he'll understand."

"No, he won't. He won't even let me speak when I say his name, I just know it. Should I tell Scarlett and then she can tell him?"

"No. It needs to be you that tells him."

I start to cry again. I've always looked up to Hunter and the thought of upsetting him like this is killing me.

"Come on, Ainsley, darling. I think you need to go to bed and stop crying. Everything will be okay. Hunter will come round."

"I know. I just hate the thought that I might upset him."

"He's a grown man. He'll get over it. He's got Scarlett now, and if he had stayed with Grace, then he wouldn't have Mixology or the life he has."

"I know. I think I just need to sleep." I get up and kiss them goodnight and then go to my bedroom in their house. I haven't stayed here for a few years, but it still feels like only yesterday.

I text Cooper,

I told Mum about you tonight. I realised I can't ignore it any longer. By the time you get home they'll all know xx Don't let me down and dump me when you get back xx

Baby I told you that isn't going to happen xx I'm going to try and wrap up my meetings quicker so that I can come home to you xx

That would be good. I have to talk to Hunter before you come home. It might be better if you're out of the country when I do. X

Yeah it might xx Let me know when you tell him and what he says xx

I will xx By the way I loved your picture earlier, but I didn't get to look at it for too long xx

Do you want another one? Xx I'm laid in bed thinking about you right now and I'm hard x

Really? Do you want to know what I'm doing? Xx

I send him a picture of my hand playing with my clit.

Oh my god baby, I wish that was my tongue.

Me too Coop xx

Cooper has been gone for four days and it's been the hardest four days of my life. I know I still have to tell Hunter about Cooper and I keep putting it off. Cooper will be home in a couple of days and I can feel the pressure closing in on me. I have always procrastinated, and I feel sick at the prospect. I'm not eating, drinking coffee all day and all night, and

I'm not sleeping either. I know I'm making myself sick and that's why I need to tell Hunter today.

We're having family dinner and I want to take the chicken way out and tell him at the same time as everyone else, purely because Scarlett will calm him down and he won't hate me as much.

I'm careful with my clothes because I don't want anyone to notice I've lost weight and start asking questions before I'm ready to tell. I make sure I'm first to arrive at Mum and Dad's and tell them what's going to happen. They said they will support me and help me as much as they can.

Everyone filters in and we help to carry the food to the table. I don't put a lot of food on my plate and it doesn't take long before Hunter notices.

"Ains, what's wrong? You not hungry today?"

"Not really."

"You don't look well. Do you need to take tonight off? You've been working really hard this week. You're always in Mixology. I'm sure you're sleeping there. We couldn't keep you in the place last week."

"I'm fine!" I snap, trying to eat my dinner.

Before he can say anything else, Scarlett reaches out and touches his hand. He stops looking at me and smiles at her.

My phone buzzes and I reach over and look at a message. It's Cooper.

Good luck Ains x I'll be home tomorrow. Let me know how it goes. X

Thanks x I just want someone to kill me right now. X

Don't talk like that. He will come around.... eventually xx

I lift my head and everyone is looking at me.

"What?" I ask, and stuff another bit of food in my mouth.

No one says anything around the table; we all eat in silence. My bad mood has filtered around everyone.

When we have cleared the dishes and are sitting down with a drink, I decide it's now or never. I have to do this or I'll be sick.

I clear my throat and everyone looks at me.

"I …" I stumble with my words. "I've got something I want to say." I look over to Mum and she smiles at me and nods.

Everyone looks up and silence shrouds the table. I clear my throat again.

"I've met someone." I say it really quickly. Hunter looks at me, as does Zac.

"What do you mean you met someone? I thought you were with Callie?" Zac says accusingly.

"Yeah, about that. We weren't together. We were pretending to get you guys off my back."

"I can't believe you lied to us. What the fuck, Ains?" Hunter says.

"What did you expect me to do? You never let a guy get close to me. You all scare them away. I didn't want to lie, but you guys were suffocating me."

Zac starts laughing. "I can't believe I've been thinking about what the two of you get up to when you leave and you just went your separate ways. That's hilarious."

Issy laughs. "I know, Zac. You were trying for us to have a threesome all the time."

He blushes and looks at Mum and Dad and shakes his head.

We all laugh.

Hunter looks at me. "So, you met someone. A guy, I presume."

"Yeah, a guy. I met him at that party I went to a couple of weeks ago and I've been with him every night since. We care about each other. He's asked me to move in with him."

"What?" Scarlett and Issy say at the same time.

"I know. Crazy, right?"

"So, why aren't you happy? Why haven't we met him yet?" Hunter asks.

"I didn't want you guys to chase him away. I wanted to keep him to myself a little bit longer."

"So, what's changed? You haven't looked happy. What did he do to you?" Hunter starts to get up from the table and Zac looks like he's going to follow him.

"SIT DOWN!" Mum says. "Let her finish. Please."

The boys sit down like they're five and being scolded. If things weren't so serious, I would laugh. But I can't.

"Are you pregnant?" Skylar asks. Everyone turns to look at him. He's so quiet, we forget about him sometimes.

I shake my head. "No, thank God. Everything is going well. He's away at the moment."

"So, why do I feel like there's something else you're not telling us?" Hunter asks. God, he is so intuitive.

I sigh.

"It's complicated." I say, not looking anyone in the eye.

"Is he married?" Zac asks. I shake my head.

"Let the girl speak," Dad says, and reaches

across and takes my hand. That small gesture brings tears to my eyes.

"I need to tell you the whole story but you need to listen to the story being going off at the deep end," I say mainly to Hunter, but look at everyone around the table.

Clearing my throat again, I start from the party. "From the moment I set eyes on him, I liked him and knew he was different from all the other guys I've been out with. Everyone called him by his nick-name and I thought it was funny, so when he asked my name, I gave myself a nickname too. We didn't need to know who the other one was. We had a strong connection and that was all we needed."

I reach out and grab my glass. My phone beeps with a message. I don't look. I can't break my flow now.

"We went out the other day to Dartmouth on his boat and he started acting strange. I told him that we have a boat in the harbour and it turns out he knows you all."

"Who is he, Ains?" Zac asks, looking like he's going to punch the head off someone.

"I'm getting to that part. Be patient."

He huffs and picks up his drink. Issy smiles at me as she rests her hand on his thigh.

"It turns out he was the one who called the ambulance for you, Hunter, when you were attacked. He stayed with you and made sure you were all right before leaving you with the ambulance. He rang the hospital to find out how you were."

"Oh my God. I need to meet him and say thank you," Hunter says, smiling.

I try to smile back, but I know that I'm going to break his heart.

"So, when he told me he saved you, he told me his name."

"Go on."

"It's Coo…" I don't even get his full name out before Hunter has jumped up from his seat and is bearing down on me from around the table.

He grabs my chair and spins me around to face him. "Are you fucking serious?"

"Hunter, sit down!" Mum says. He ignores her.

"Don't tell me you fell for his charm like Grace did? He's using you, Ainsley. He's trying to come between us. He doesn't really want you, he just wants to get back at me."

I can't take anymore. I push him away from me and I stand up, proud and tall. I poke him in his chest.

"Not everything is about you, Hunter. You need to get off that fucking high pedestal you put yourself on and take a look around you." I poke him again. "The world doesn't revolve around you." Poke. "He likes me for me. He didn't know who I was and I didn't know who he was." Poke. "My life has fallen apart since I found out."

Hunter stands there, dumbfounded. "You want to continue to see him, don't you?"

"Yes. He wants me to move in with him and I'm considering it."

"Are you fucking joking?" Zac stands up and joins Hunter.

I roll my eyes. "Not you as well, Zac."

"Everyone sit down!" Dad says. He stands up and moves towards the two boys. "Sit down and behave like the men you really are. Not stupid boys. We've brought you all up to listen to each other and help each other. We are a tight family and we intend to stay that way."

Hunter looks at me, shakes his head, and walks over to his side of the table. I think he's going to sit down, but he doesn't. He pushes his chair in. "That's me out! I don't want to look at you right now, Ainsley. Don't come into work. You're not wanted."

I gasp.

He looks down at Scarlett. "Are you coming with me or not?" She looks at me and mouths, 'Sorry.' She stands and leaves with him.

Zac does the same and Issy goes with him.

Skylar is the only one who stays at the table.

I can't help myself; I break down. I start crying hysterically. I can't control my tears and sobs.

"Baby, it will be okay. Hunter and Zac will come around. They just need to get over the shock," Dad says, pulling me into a hug.

"Yeah, they weren't expecting it. Hunter doesn't mean what he says. It's just a shock," Skylar says, ever the innocent.

"I know. But he told me he didn't want me there." Sobbing, I can't speak anymore.

My phone starts ringing in my hand and I see Cooper's face on the screen. I turn it over. I can't talk to him right now. Mum reaches over, takes the phone, and slides it to take the call.

I reach out to grab it back, but she shakes her head and walks into the kitchen.

6

KISS ON THE LIPS

1 1/2oz peach schnapps, 5oz frozen mango mix, 1 tbsp grenadine, 2 cups crushed ice

COOPER

"**A**insley. Are you okay? You didn't answer my texts. Ainsley, baby, answer me." I'm frantic. I need to know how she got on. I haven't been able to concentrate on anything since I knew she was going to tell her family.

"Cooper, this is Verity. Firstly, Ainsley is okay, but she's upset. Secondly, I'm sorry for the way my family has treated you. We didn't give you the chance to explain yourself and we should have."

"It's okay. I know how close the James family is.

I'm sorry I seem to be causing trouble again. How is she? I wish I could be there with her."

I don't care what she thinks about me. I need Ainsley.

"She'll be okay. We'll look after her tonight. I don't think she should be alone. When are you home, Cooper?"

"I'm trying to get home tomorrow if I can. I want to be there for her. I want to take care of her. I love her, Verity. I can't believe she's come into my life."

"I'm glad you're serious about her because what she just did could tear her relationship with her brothers apart."

"I know, and I told her that I would walk away if she wanted me to. It would be hard, but if it means she and Hunter keep their relationship, then I'll do it."

"I know. I see how her face lights up when she gets a text from you or when she's talking about you. Just treat her right, Cooper. That's all I ask. I have to go and see if she's all right now, but hurry home. She needs you."

She hangs up and I'm beside myself. Ainsley has just done the hardest thing in the world and I'm not there for her. I need to leave here and get home to her as soon as I can.

Leaving my hotel room, I rush down to reception. "I want to check out in the morning, please."

"Is everything okay, sir?" the receptionist asks, looking into my eyes. She blinks and smiles at me. I think she's flirting with me, but I have no interest.

"I have to get home to my wife." That will throw her off. I stop and smile. I like the sound of that. My wife. Hmm, who would have thought?

"Okay, sir. Thank you for your stay." She turns to make a note on the computer. I turn and walk out of the hotel. Taking my phone, I ring Johnson.

"Hey, can we meet now? I need to wrap everything up. I have to go home tomorrow."

"Really? I thought we had another couple of days to firm up all the details." He sounds angry.

I really don't care if I lose his business, to be honest. Ainsley means more to me than his company.

"Yeah, sorry. Something cropped up and I need to go back home to deal with it. I'd stay if I could."

"Okay. Come over now and let's work for the next few hours and then we can finish when you get home." He sighs and hangs up.

Grabbing a cab, I give him Johnson's address,

and while I'm in the back of the cab, I send Ainsley a text.

Hey baby. I'm coming home early.

I don't get a response and, to be honest, I don't expect one. For the next five hours, Johnson and I concentrate on his brand and hash everything out. It's three in the morning when I get back to my hotel room. Packing my bag, I smile to myself, thinking of Ainsley and how much I want to see her.

I eventually manage to get to sleep but only for a few hours before I have to check out and get to the airport. I was lucky there was a morning flight that had space. All the way home, I think about her and what she's going through. I don't care what Hunter says to me as long as he doesn't upset Ainsley. I've never felt like this about anyone before. I feel territorial. Like if he hurts her then he's hurting me.

When I land in Bristol, I jump in my car and make my way down the motorway on my two-hour journey. I try to ring Ainsley, but her phone is turned off. I'm hoping she's not on her own, so when I get to Torquay, I head in the direction of Verity's house. I haven't been there in many years, but I know the way, having been a regular visitor in their house.

When I pull into the drive, I smile when I see Ainsley's car. Luckily, Hunter's bike isn't there.

I abandon my car and run up to the front door, knocking wildly.

"Okay, okay. I'm coming," I hear as someone walks towards the door. "Cooper. I'm not sure it's a pleasure, but if you can cheer Ainsley up then I will be forever grateful." Jack throws the door open wide for me to walk in.

"Thanks, Jack. Where is she?"

He points to the conservatory. I walk past Verity with a nod of my head and walk into the room which looks out across the ocean. I always loved this room. It's always flooded with light. I find Ainsley sitting in the big arm chair which has the best view.

I run up and kneel in front of her. Touching her hand, I say, "Hey, baby. I'm here now."

She looks up at me and starts to sob. "What? What are you doing here? You need to go before Hunter comes." Then she takes a breath. "You're really here?"

Standing, I lift her and sit down in the comfy chair with her on my lap. She curls herself up into a ball on my lap and I wrap my arms around her as she sobs. My heart breaks just a little bit more.

When she has stopped crying and seems to be breathing better, I put my finger under her chin and make her look at me. She smiles at me.

"Hey," she says, blushing.

"Hey." I lean in and gently kiss her.

Verity comes in and clears her throat. "Thank you for coming, Cooper. You've shown us how important she is to you by dropping everything and coming home to her."

"I asked her to come with me. I didn't want to leave her for so long. I missed her." Ainsley snuggles in further to my chest.

"I can see that." Verity laughs. "Things have been tense here since she told Hunter about you. I wasn't sure your reasons for seeing her were honourable." Ainsley moans into my chest. Verity continues, "But I can see now that you fell for her before you knew who she was."

"I sure did. From the first moment I saw her I knew she was special. I'm sorry for the pain I caused your family back then and now. I tried to talk to Hunter. To tell him what actually happened, but he was so stubborn."

She laughs. "Yeah, he still is."

"I know. I'll do whatever it takes to make it right between us. I intend to be in Ainsley's life for a long time so we need to sort this out man to man."

She nods. "Yes, you do. Take care of my daughter, Cooper," she says as she leaves the room.

We sit in silence for a while just watching the sun setting and the stars coming out. "Let's go home," I say, kissing Ainsley on the top of her head.

She looks up at me and smiles for the first time since I arrived. "Yeah. Let's go home." She climbs off my lap and holds her hand out to help me up.

As we walk out of the room and into the dining room, Jack stands and walks over to me. He takes me into a hug. "Welcome back. Thank you for helping Hunter when you found him. You could have just walked by after the way he - we all - treated you. Thank you."

"Hunter was my best friend for more years than he hasn't been. I would never walk past him and I believe he would have done the same for me — regardless of the circumstances."

He nods. Ainsley says goodnight to them both and we jump into my car. Driving back to my house, I can't let go of her hand. I just want to keep contact.

I help her out of the car and then carry her into

my house. She doesn't react, just snuggles in. Carrying her straight to the bedroom, I lay her down gently on the bed. "Get in, baby. I'm going to have a shower and then I want to snuggle. We can talk in the morning." I kiss her on the cheek and walk into the en-suite.

I have the quickest shower in the history of showers, and when I walk into my bedroom and see her under my covers, my heart flips.

She pulls the covers back for me to climb in, and when I'm settled, I pull her into my side. "I love you Ainsley. You're mine and no one is going to change that. Not even Hunter."

"Yours," she says as she drifts off into a peaceful sleep. My body is so happy to be close to her that it doesn't take long before I fall asleep wrapped around her.

7

LOVE BITE

1oz cherry liqueur, 1oz orange liqueur, 1oz cream

AINSLEY

Stretching in the bed, my feet meet resistance. Turning to face the resistance, I see Cooper smiling at me. I smile back and roll into his open arms. "Morning," I say kissing his chest.

"Morning, baby. Did you sleep well?" he asks gruffly.

"I sure did. Best sleep all week."

"I know that feeling." He tightens his arms around me.

"Watch it. You'll squeeze me to death." I chuckle.

He releases his arms slightly.

"Did your work finish early? Is that why you came home?"

"No. I came home because you needed me. I shouldn't have left you alone when you had to tell Hunter. That was cowardly of me."

"No. I had to tell him, not you."

"Yeah, but I should have been there for you afterwards. I wrapped everything up and got the next plane home."

I kiss him gently on the lips. "Thank you."

We lay like that for a while. Not speaking. Just existing. Together. Those moments mean more than the sexual moments, in my book.

"Let's get some food," Cooper says. "I've not eaten for a long time." He moves his arms open so I can crawl out of bed and we head into the kitchen.

I'm sitting at the kitchen bench while Cooper is cooking breakfast. The coffee pot is gurgling in the background, giving out the best smell in the world. "So, are you going to Mixology today?" he asks.

"Yeah. I have to. I need to make sure he listens to me."

"Do you want me to talk to him? It's time we had it out."

"I know. I just need to talk to him first and then you can talk to him. Is that okay?"

"Of course it is. If that's what you want, then I'm behind you all the way." He walks around the bench. "Actually, I like being behind you." He kisses the back of my neck. He gently pushes me forward so my arse is slightly off the stool. He leans over me, pressing his body against me, and I can feel his hard cock in the cheeks of my arse. I moan and turn my head slightly.

"Are you trying to burn the bacon?" I ask, smiling at him.

"No. I just want you, Ainsley. I want to crawl inside you and never leave."

"I'd like that a lot, but right now. I'm hungry," I say, sitting back down on my stool with a huff.

He laughs and swings the stool around so I'm facing him. He grasps my face with his hands and devours me. When he eventually pulls away, I want more. I want him to carry me away, but he touches my nose with his finger and smiles as he walks back around the bench to finish cooking the bacon.

Even though I'm really hungry, I can't eat very much. My mind is on what I need to do today. I can't put it off or let it fester. I need to talk to

Hunter, and once I've got through it, then Cooper can talk to him.

We get dressed after breakfast and Cooper insists on driving me down to Mixology. I know everyone is there and I have work to do. He leans across and kisses me. "I'm staying here. If you need me, just text, and I'll be there to kick his arse. I always could beat him down."

I smile. I know he's only trying to make me feel better, but this is something I need to do myself.

"I'll be fine. He's my brother. He won't physically hurt me, but he can hurt me with his words. I'll text you when I've spoken to him." I kiss him, take a deep breath, and get out of his car. Walking across the road, I open the front door to Mixology and walk in.

As I step into the bar, Zac is the first one to see me.

"Ainsley, what're you doing here?"

"I work here," I say, looking around the bar to see if I can see Hunter.

"He won't be pleased to see you."

"I doubt he will. But I'm his sister and he needs to listen to what I have to say." I barge my way into the office and take a deep breath.

Issy is sitting on the couch, Scarlett is sitting at

her desk, and Hunter is pacing furiously. They all turn their heads to stare at me when I walk in.

"What the fuck are you doing here?" Hunter shouts.

"I work here. I have work to do. This bar won't run itself, you know."

He looks at me and I can see the temper rising in him. His face starts to get red and he looks at the other two girls. The door opens behind me and Zac steps inside.

"You're fired!" Hunter says, and starts to walk to the door.

Scarlett shouts at him to stop. He doesn't, he opens the door. I suddenly find my voice.

"You're firing me because I'm happy with someone?" I spit at him.

"No, I'm firing you because you betrayed me."

"Fuck you. You need to give Cooper a chance to tell you his side of the story. You disappeared before you gave him the chance to tell you what happened. Is that what you intend doing every time something happens that you don't like?" I poke him in the chest.

"Ainsley, Hunter, you both need to calm down," Scarlett says.

"No, Scarlett. I am sick to death of my brothers.

They won't let me see a guy because they want to believe I'm a virgin. Well, let me tell you this here and now, I am not a virgin. I lost my virginity on your couch, Hunter, to your best friend, Ed. So stick that in your fucking pipe and smoke it."

Hunter takes a step back. "I'll fucking kill him!"

I see Scarlett smile. "Babe, calm down. You didn't really think she was a virgin, did you?"

He turns to look at her. "It doesn't matter what I thought. That doesn't change anything." He turns back to look at me. "Are you still here?"

I shake my head. "You make me laugh, Hunter. You think you're the big I am, but you ran away with your tail between your legs and expected us all to wait for you to lick your wounds and come back. Grace was a bitch. She tried it on with everyone but you were too blind to see it. She was horrible to Mum and Dad and you don't even want to know what she said to me. But in your eyes, she could do no wrong." I step up closer to him. "Maybe you ran away because you knew there was truth in her behaviour. Maybe you didn't want to face the fact that she was a bitch. You didn't give us a chance to be there for you. You just ran. We were the ones who had to look after Mum and Dad when you left. When Mum cried because you didn't speak to us, who do you think looked after her? Me, that's who! Did you ever stop to think about how your selfish behaviour affected anyone else?" I look up into his eyes. "No. You fucking didn't."

I step backwards and sit on the couch. I'm exhausted, both mentally and physically.

"Even after the way you treated Cooper, he still stopped to make sure you were all right and put you in the ambulance and even checked on you. Would you have done that to him? He thinks you would. I don't think so at all, you selfish prick!"

He doesn't say anything, he just looks at me. Scarlett is at his side, holding onto his arm. I see her rubbing it.

I jump up. "Actually, do you know something? I don't want to work here with you bunch of fucking arseholes." I look at the two girls. "Sorry, I don't mean you, but these two Neanderthals. I'd rather be around people who care about me and not just themselves. Do you know how much I sobbed when you left the other night? I didn't sleep because I was worried about you. Do you know what Cooper did? He got on the first plane he could and raced home to make sure I was okay. He wanted to be there with me because he knew what a bastard you were going to be. That is what you do when you love someone."

I open the door and wait for a fraction to see if anyone stops me. They don't. I don't turn around. I don't want them to see how upset I am. I don't make a noise. I just have silent tears running down my face. "You can stick your job up your fucking hole. You know where to find me if you ever want your sister back."

I walk out of the office, down the corridor, through the bar, and out of the front door. Cooper sees me and he runs across the road. I fall into him and cry.

"I'll fucking kill him," he says, trying to get inside Mixology.

"Thanks, Cooper, but he's not worth it. Take me home."

CORPSE REVIVER

¾ oz gin, ¾ oz lemon juice, ¾ Cointreau, ¾ oz Lillet, 1
dash absinthe

COOPER

I could fucking kill Hunter for what he's doing to my beautiful woman. She won't eat. She won't stop crying, and she won't leave the house. Her mum and dad have been up to my house to see her. Even they can't get through to her. It's been a week since she confronted Hunter and she needs to stop moping around.

"Ainsley, can you come into my office for a minute?" I shout out to her. I hear her trudging down the corridor and I smile to myself. The closer she gets, the faster my heart beats. I love her so much. I would do anything for her. Right now, she needs me to be strong for her.

She pokes her head around the door.

"Come on in," I say, patting my leg. "Take a seat." I wink at her. She smiles and sits on my lap.

"Were you looking for me?" she asks innocently.

"I was. I need to pick your brain. Look at this concept here. It just isn't right and I don't know what I'm missing."

Her smile drops slightly when she realises I want to talk about work and then she looks at my computer screen.

We spend the next hour thrashing out ideas about the branding. She has some amazing ideas. Work has never been so much fun. When we finalise the ideas, I send a report off to the business owner, and just as I'm finishing, she comes in with a coffee.

"Thank you. I needed that distraction. Can I help you with any other projects?" she asks, looking towards my computer.

A thought hits me right at that moment. I'm not sure what she's going to say when I ask her, but I think it would be perfect.

"Ainsley, you're amazing. You have some great ideas. Would you like to go into partnership with me? I do marketing and branding, but I'm not great with the whole organizing side of things and outsource a great deal of my work to other companies, especially for event planning. You know, for launches and stuff. You would be fantastic at it. The events you've organised at Mixology have been amazing and you don't get enough credit for it."

She sits down beside me and stares at me. "Do you really think I won't be able to work at Mixology again?" she asks. "Do you think Hunter won't ever speak to me again?" I can see her heart breaking as she thinks about not having him in her life. Their family has always been close and this is the first time they've had a big argument.

"No, baby," I say, taking her hand. "Hunter would be a fool to not talk to you. He would be a fool to let you leave Mixology. But I'm talking about what you want. What does Ainsley James want to do with her life? Do you want to work at Mixology for the rest of your life?"

She shakes her head. "I hadn't really thought about it, but I suppose I don't want to be there forever. Anyway, I don't work there anymore, so it's not an option."

"Look, we both know Hunter will come around at some stage and you'll be working there again in a week. Just think about what you want in life. This is your chance to do something for yourself."

"What if we do go into partnership? What if we split up? What happens then?"

"Baby, how many times do I have to tell you? I'm not letting you walk away from me. I would follow you to the ends of the Earth. You are my future, and without you in it, it's not worth anything."

She climbs on my lap. "I love you, Cooper." She takes my face in between her hands and kisses me gently. "I want to be wherever you are. I'd love to work with you. I'm not sure I'm ready to give up on Mixology quite yet, but that chance has been taken away from me. Let's do this." She smiles and my heart jumps with joy.

I lift her up and she straddles my waist as I carry her through to our bedroom. I throw her on the bed and lean over her. As I start to take her clothes off, the doorbell rings. I ignore it. I take off her top. Ring ring. Then I start to take her leggings off. Ring ring. *Who the fuck is that?* I kiss her. Ring ring.

She giggles. "You'd better get it." She pulls her leggings back up as I straighten myself up and walk out to the front door, ready to tear strips off whoever is on the other side.

"What do you want?" I growl as I open the door.

"I want to talk."

I didn't expect Hunter to be there.

"Hang on a minute," I say, closing the door in his face.

"Who is it?" Ainsley asks, walking towards me.

"It's Hunter."

Her face drops. "Is he here to see me?"

I shake my head. "No. He wants to talk to me. I don't want you to be upset. Do you want to go to your mum's and I'll collect you when he's gone?"

She nods and goes to put her shoes on. As I open the door to let her out, she walks past Hunter without saying a word.

He reaches out to grab her arm, "Ains." She doesn't even look at him. I smile as she climbs into her car and tears out of the driveway. I know inside she must be freaking out, but she doesn't show him that she's hurting.

I step aside and let Hunter in and then close the door behind him.

Neither of us says anything until I show him

into the kitchen. "Do you want coffee?" I ask, because I hate awkward silences.

"Thanks," he says as he sits on the stool.

He doesn't say anything while I make the coffee, but I can see him in the reflection of the cooker hood and he's checking out my house. I'm proud of how far I've come.

"Nice place you have here," Hunter says as I hand him his coffee.

"Yeah. I worked hard for it. You're not here to check out my house, so how about we start talking?"

He takes a sip of his coffee and then looks me in the eye.

"I'm sorry. I should have given you the chance to tell me your side of the situation and not run off. Ainsley told me I was a coward by running away from everyone and everything. She's right. I didn't want to face up to Grace's behaviour and it was easier to block it all out."

"Yeah, you were a coward. I was so pissed off when you wouldn't talk to me. Are you ready to hear it all now?" I ask, searching his face for signs that he might just get up and walk out.

He nods.

So I tell him about what really happened that night and then I tell him the rest.

"Grace had been trying it on with a few people at the party while you were being the gracious host. I saw her trying to kiss Jonathan West. Do you remember him?"

"Yes. He was always a snake. Did he kiss her?"

"No. I went up to her and reminded her you were there. I heard rumours all night about her, saying she had been sleeping around and that you were a mug for putting up with her. When she disappeared, I went looking for you and her. I went into your room and she was laid on the bed, naked. At first I thought she thought I was you, but then she said my name and I realised what she was doing. I was telling her to get some clothes on and that I was going to tell you everything I had heard that night when you walked in and everything exploded. I had your back that night as I always have."

"You didn't kiss her then?"

"No. I never did. She was so afraid you were going to dump her and that's why she said what she did. After you left, she tried to convince me that it meant we could be together, but I told her I never wanted to see her. I told her she was so far off my radar it wasn't funny."

I take a big sip of my coffee that's now going

cold. "When you wouldn't take my calls, I tried to ring your mum, but she wouldn't talk to me. She believed your side of the story and I even tried to call around, but your dad or Zac would always block me."

He smiles, probably thinking of Zac trying to be the hard man even though he was only young.

"I tried so many times to talk to you, but you didn't want to know me. When I saw you on the ground a couple of months ago, I knew I had to help you. It didn't matter what had happened between us, you were still my best mate."

"Thank you for calling the ambulance and waiting. I remember listening to someone say my name, but I was in and out of consciousness. I'm not sure I would have done the same in the circumstances."

"Yes, you would. You're not a bad person, Hunter. You never were."

"I feel bad for how I treated you, but even more so about Ainsley. It's weird to see her with a guy she likes. We tried to stop her seeing guys and she even had to pretend to be a lesbian."

I nod. Ainsley had told me and I thought it was funny.

"You did say some horrible things to her. She is in a lot of pain right now. She looks up to you and respects you and you told her you didn't want her around anymore."

"I know. Scarlett went nuts with me. She told me I was a selfish, egotistical prick."

"Well, we all know that's true. Scarlett obviously knows you well."

Hunter laughs. "She sure does. She is one of Ainsley's best friends. I just hope I haven't ruined my relationship with Ainsley. She means the world to me."

"I know she does. I love her. When we met, we didn't know who the other was. We clicked and got serious very fast. I know she's your sister but I want you to know that I won't hurt her."

"I trust you, Cooper. She's precious and I wouldn't trust anyone else to take care of her." He reaches out and touches my shoulder, then he opens his arms for a man hug.

It's not awkward at all. I lean in and we do that thump on the back of the shoulder thing that men do when they think they're being emotional.

"Now we have to mend your relationship with your sister."

"Too right we do." He smiled at me.

AINSLEY

Holy crap. When Cooper said Hunter was at the door, I could hardly breathe. Walking past him hurt so much, and then when he reached out to touch me, I just couldn't stop. He needed to know he hurt me.

Sitting at Mum and Dad's though, waiting to see what happened after I left, is horrendous. It seems like days pass before I hear a car turn into the drive. Mum was really good and listened to me crying and told me that everything would be alright.

Apparently, Dad had stepped in and spoken to Hunter. Dad never gets involved, but when he does, we know things are serious.

Mum holds my hand as Hunter lets himself in the front door. He doesn't look like he has a black eye or anything. Maybe they didn't fight. I see movement just behind him and Cooper walks in and closes the door behind him.

He smiles at me and I release a breath I didn't realise I was holding. He moves past Hunter and stands next to me. "Hey, baby. Everything is fine."

Hunter moves closer to me. "I'm sorry, Ains. Once again, I only thought of myself. I was mad because you were sneaking around and made us believe you and Callie were a couple."

"You know why that was though, don't you?"

"Yes. I'm sorry. You're my baby sister and I don't want some prick upsetting you. I know I'm that prick right now and I'll do whatever it takes to apologise. Then, when you said Cooper's name, I just saw red and thought you were doing it to spite me somehow. Scarlett made me realise that that's not the case. I didn't give Cooper the chance all those years ago and I've apologised for that, but I don't want to lose my sister when I've just gained a friend."

Wow, he really is feeling sorry for himself. "Some of those things can't be unsaid, Hunter. You said them, and deep down somewhere, you meant them."

"No, that's just it. I didn't mean them. You mean more to me than anything. I talk to you about everything, we work together so well, and I miss you so much." He reaches out for me. "I'm sorry. I'm such a stubborn bastard." He takes me into a hug and I cry.

"Hunter, you hurt me." I sob into his shoulder.

"I know and I'm so sorry." He cradles my head and rubs his hand across the back of my hair. "I'll make it up to you, I promise. Just forgive me, Ains. I love you."

"I forgive you, but I can't forget straight away."

"That's all I can ask for right now," he says as he pulls away from me. "I'm so sorry and I'm thankful too."

"Why would you be thankful that we fell out?" I ask, puzzled.

"Because you brought Cooper back into my life. Thank you. I've missed him over the years, but I've been too stubborn to do anything about it." He looks over to Cooper. Hunter walks over to Cooper. "Sorry, mate."

Cooper smiles, and seeing them together like that makes me smile too. They look like they did back in school.

Cooper walks over to me, puts his arm around my shoulders, and pulls me close, kissing me on my cheek as he does. "I know this looks strange to you, Hunter, but Ainsley is it for me. She makes me feel happy and like I've come home. I love her and I'm happy you're on board with all of this."

"Yeah, I am," Hunter says, not really looking at us. I guess he still has a problem seeing me with a man.

"Good, I'm glad," I say, looking at Hunter. "Because I have something else to tell you."

"You're not pregnant, are you?" Hunter shouts, looking daggers at Cooper.

I laugh. "No. I'm not stupid. You know how I quit my job the other day?"

"Yeah, but it's yours and I assume you're coming back to me."

"I kind of got another job." I say, quietly. "Cooper and I are going into partnership." I hold my hands up at Hunter. "Before you start kicking off, let me explain."

Hunter sits down. "Okay, explain, because I don't like the sound of this."

I laugh. "You never were one for change. Cooper has his own company where he does branding and marketing for companies across the world. He outsources a lot of the work for events and marketing to other companies, which obviously costs him money. However, with my event planning and marketing experience from Mixology. he has asked me to work with him. Before you start getting upset and shouting at me, I can still do events for Mixology. I know you won't be able to handle it anyway." I laugh. "Scarlett is very capable in the office and knows how to do everything. Issy is there all the time too and she can help out. I'm always going to be at the end of the phone to help out when you need me to. I wouldn't abandon you all together."

"Wow, kick me while I'm down, Ains," Hunter says. "I knew you would leave us one day. You've always been too good for Mixology, but I didn't want to tell you that because you would leave. I thought you would have moved into marketing and moved to Bristol or somewhere like that. I guess I should be grateful that you're staying in Torquay." He stands and comes over to Cooper and me. "I'm really happy for you both. Cooper, look after her. I will kick your arse if you don't." He laughs. "Does that mean you aren't working tonight, Ainsley?"

I laugh out loud. "I'll work tonight and I'll keep working in Mixology until we can sort everything out with you and with Cooper's company. How does that sound?"

"That sounds perfect. Thank you."

We all leave and Cooper takes me home. Yes, his house is my home too. Actually, wherever he is, is where my heart is.

EPILOGUE

COOPER

We're all sitting around the table, waiting for Skylar to turn up. Apparently he is never late and never comes in last, according to Ainsley. I take the time to look around the table and see how this family has grown since I first became a part of it. Back then, Skylar was a baby. He was always a quiet kid, but I really liked playing with him.

It's strange seeing the other girls around the table. Scarlett is gorgeous and such a nice girl. She has been around to our house quite a lot with Hunter and to spend time with Ainsley. She is really funny and she can handle Hunter, which makes me laugh. He is madly in love with her and would do anything for her.

The funniest thing to watch is Zac with Issy. She is tiny compared to him. He is huge; his muscles have muscles, if you know what I mean. Izzy has him wrapped around her little finger. He would do anything for her. I know he has been through a lot and he could have stayed on a path of self-destruction, but, luckily for him, Issy didn't let him.

I wish I could spend some time with Keaton. They've all been telling me how funny he is. Dakota sounds like a right laugh and their love story is great. We're all hoping to go out to Australia to see them in the World Surfing Championships if we can.

Verity and Jack haven't changed a bit. They're still an amazing couple, and if Ainsley and I have half the life they have, then we will be doing well. Looking around the table makes me realise I want a family with Ainsley. I want what she has had all her life. She looks at me and smiles. I wonder if she knows what I'm thinking.

"So, Cooper, it's so good having you with us at the table. I know we've apologized already and this will be the last time, but we are truly sorry that we all treated you wrongly," Verity says.

I hold up my hands. "Please, there's no need to apologise. If Hunter hadn't left then he wouldn't have Mixology. I probably wouldn't be with Ainsley, because she would have been Hunter's annoying younger sister." I look at Ainsley. She gives me a sharp dig in the ribs. "Ow. I always liked her, but didn't think I'd be able to date her."

She leans into me. "Aw, thanks."

"So, tell us about your business venture. What're you and Ainsley doing?"

I spend the next ten minutes or so telling them about our marketing and event company. Asking Ainsley to work with me has been the best decision I've ever made, except to date her, of course.

We are then interrupted by the front door opening. "I'm home!" Everyone turns to watch Skylar walk through the door. "Sorry I'm late," he says as he walks over to his seat at the table and sits down. He looks around and reaches out to take some food. "What did I miss?"

"Skylar James, where are your manners? Nobody is late for Sunday dinner unless you apologise in advance," Verity says, staring at him.

"Erm... sorry," he stutters.

We all eat in silence. The whole atmosphere has changed.

When we've eaten lunch and dessert, we clear the dishes away and retire to the conservatory. Jack says, "Skylar, why were you late? What's going on?"

"I'm sorry. I just got a phone call telling me that I've been accepted into a competition for Young VJ of the Year. this is huge for me. The call went on longer than I expected."

Everyone starts talking at once. "Well done, Sky. You deserve it," Ainsley says, and reaches out for my hand.

"Why don't you look so happy about it?" Verity asks.

"*If* I get through to the finals, which I probably won't, they are on when the World Surfing Championships are on and it means I wouldn't be able to go to Australia with you all."

"Sky, this is far more important to your career than going to Australia," Hunter says.

"I know, but the World Surfing Championships is the biggest thing that has happened to our family. I can't miss seeing my brother in that competition." Skylar might be the quiet one, but he is the one who loves when the family are together. I can see his leg bouncing up and down as he thinks about missing Keaton and Dakota's competition. The fact that he would give up his dream job to see his brother in his competition shows what kind of guy he is.

"Sometimes you have to make decisions in your life that you don't like, but invariably they turn out to be the best decisions you make," Jack says.

"I just don't know what to do." He shakes his head.

"You'll work something out," Verity says.

Ainsley stands up. "Come on, Cooper. Let's go home. Mum, dinner was lovely as usual. Hunter, Zac, girls, see you all tonight."

We leave, and when we pull up to our home, we walk silently out to the back and sit with the lights on. I grab a glass of wine for each of us and pick up two blankets on the way out. We sit there silently, with the blankets wrapped around us, sipping our wine and just being.

"I enjoyed today," I say quietly, not wanting to spoil the peace and quiet.

"Me too. I enjoyed it more than ever because you were there with me."

I reach out and take her hand. "I love you. I hope you know that."

"I love you too," she says.

"Good," I say. "Because our journey in life is just beginning and nothing will stop us."

Who knew a few months ago when I was just surviving and coasting along in my life that it would get changed so much by this amazing, beautiful, headstrong woman?

Not me, that's for sure!

The end

THANK YOU

Thank you for reading **AINSLEY** as part of the standalone Mixology. I really hope you enjoyed it and that you'll consider leaving a review on Amazon. It's a great way to help other readers discover new books. Click here to leave a review.

If you like **AINSLEY** and would like to read more, turn the page for a list of my other books. And if you don't want to miss any future releases, please join my newsletter here.

BETSEY – Book 4 in the Whiskey Sour standalone series.

Betsey is a living, breathing, fifties chick. She loves

the movies, the songs, the clothes and the lifestyle. She's a nurse who looks after anyone that she can. Her Grampy is sick, and she does what she can to help him and make him comfortable.

Billie is gorgeous, funny and extremely sexy. Wearing slick clothes, leather jackets, telling jokes and singing songs, Billie is the newest member of the Whiskey Sour team.

After a traumatic experience Betsey doesn't want any man to touch her but, somehow, she's attracted to Billie and doesn't understand it.

Follow their story of forbidden love, rejection and heartbreak for the ones that they love.

Warning: There are extremely tasteful and sensual scenes of F/F which are vital to the story, if this offends you then please do not read.

ACKNOWLEDGMENTS

Once again thank you to all my readers for taking time out of their busy lives to read one of my books. It seriously amazes me how everyone loves my words. I try to put a small piece of me into each of the books that I write. A lot of AINSLEY's wit and humour comes from my own sarcasm. I love the MIXOLOGY series and will be sad when it ends with Skylar.

Thank you to my editor Kyra Lennon for fine tuning my book to make it better to read. You always do such great work with my books and I am so thankful to have you beside me.

My PA, Natasha, you are always there for me and

talk me down on the ledge so many times, thank you. Jen, you are never too far away and you help me so much with my social media that I need to thank you for helping to make me more visible so that people can see my books in the first place.

JC, your formatting is the bomb!

Kirsty from <u>The Pretty Little Design Boutique</u> thank you so much for this gorgeous cover. I love all the Mixology covers, but I will admit this is my favourite. I can't wait to see what you do with the next one!

Finally, a thank you to my friend, Karen. You know who you are and you're there when I need to run ideas past you and you usually message me when I need it the most. It's like you feel my emotions and for that I am grateful.

Hope you have enjoyed Ainsley and I look forward to bringing you Skylar next year.

ABOUT THE AUTHOR

I hated English at school! Really hated it! I gave up on English Literature in fourth year because I hated writing stories; couldn't make them up to save my life. I hated writing precis and I was horrendous at grammar. Having lived in Norway when I was younger, English was my second language.

When I received my iPad six years ago I started reading on the kindle app and wrote to an author about how much I enjoyed her book. That opened up the whole facebook author world to me. I started reviewing books (ironic, right?) and then started beta reading (even more ironic) after pointing out some big mistakes in a book plot I was reviewing before release.

I realised I had a story in me, yeah I know everyone says that, but I really believed I did. Thirteen books later …. Welcome to the world of Krissy V!

Worse, In Sickness and In Health, To Love and To
Cherish)

To Have or To Hold – Standalone in Till Death Us Do
Part Series

For Richer or For Poorer – Standalone in Till Death Us
Do Part Series

CHOCOLATE BOX ROMANCE

Beauty Within

0-Love in 6 Minutes

A Taste of Christmas Dublin Style

ROMANTIC COMEDY

Eff This Diet – Standalone

SUSHINE TOUR Series

Sunshine in Madrid

Sunshine at Christmas